The Violent Breed

Benton City suited Gabe Parker for both had one thing in common – a past they were keen to forget. So Gabe stopped running and settled down, and contented himself with bringing up a family and running a gunsmith's shop.

The quiet life for Gabe was soon shattered by the sudden arrival of George, needing a gun to protect the valuable loot he had hidden in his belt. In George's wake follow the Coyotes who, ruthless and lawless, will do anything to lay hands on George's prize. Benton City quickly becomes engulfed in violence and death as the brutal outlaws wreak havoc on the peaceful town.

Vicious killings and the sight of an old enemy spur Gabe into action, and he buckles on his guns for the last time . . . but is it too late to defend not only George, but also his family? Only time – and his guns would tell!

The Violent Breed

Graham Hawk

A Black Horse Western

ROBERT HALE · LONDON

© Vic J. Hanson 1963, 2003
First hardcover edition 2003
Originally published in paperback as
The Violent Breed by Chuck Adams

ISBN 0 7090 7286 4

Robert Hale Limited
Clerkenwell House
Clerkenwell Green
London EC1R 0HT

Typeset by
Derek Doyle & Associates, Liverpool.
Printed and bound in Great Britain by
Antony Rowe Limited, Wiltshire

ONE

THE STRANGER
BUYS A GUN

Gabe Parker sighted along the barrel of the rifle, decided it was straight and true, beautifully assembled. He shot the bolt home and placed the rifle beside the other two on his bench.

The sun streamed through the dust-dappled window and burnished the barrels and the walnut stocks. A beautiful sight, thought Gabe. Guns were his life; his gunsmith's shop; that and his wife, Kate, and his daughter Prunella.

A shadow fell across the sunlight. Gabe looked up, feeling the old tension in the calves of his legs.

Instinctively, he almost lifted the rifle again. Then he checked himself, realising the weapon was unloaded anyway.

His lips curled sardonically. He was a gunsmith with no loaded gun to protect him. His dirty white apron concealed nothing more dangerous than a clasp knife, a pipe and pouch.

The man had entered silently through the open door, had moved across the window. And now he stood still, watching

5

Gabe. Because he had his back to the light Gabe could not see his face. He was tall and lean and straight. Young, or youngish, obviously. Wary as a cat. So many of them were like this: Gabe was a little wearied by the thought. The young ones, the running ones, the wild ones. The dangerous ones with a love for guns that was an unhealthy love.

Was this another one of that kind?

But there were so many kinds after all. And they were all his customers, his livelihood.

'Can I help you, suh?' he asked in his soft Texas drawl.

'I want a good handgun,' said the man. He moved then, came nearer.

Gabe saw that his holster was empty. Worn low. Tied to the thigh by a whang-string, the sagging pouch looked like a silly mouth. It didn't look right that way: it certainly needed filling.

'You've come to the right place, suh.' This was Gabe's favourite phrase.

'I've got all sorts,' he added as he turned towards his racks.

But he did not turn his back completely on his visitor. He had money here as well as guns and ammunition. A peaceable man, he was also an inherently wary one. A gaping holster could speak a lie: the man might have a derringer concealed somewhere, or maybe a knife.

Gabe had noted also that though the visitor looked like a cowhand he didn't wear the usual scuffed high-heeled boots, but soft moccasins, so that he moved softly, almost catlike.

Then he was bellying up to the bench and Gabe, two guns in each big hand, had a chance for a better look at him.

He was even younger than Gabe had expected him to be. Little more than a boy. A thin wedge-shaped face. A tight consciously-tough mouth. Locks of lank pale hair escaping from beneath the floppy brim of a dirty grey Stetson.

6

Gabe could not see his eyes because they were downcast. Their gaze was fixed on the four guns as Gabe placed them now on the bench, fan-shaped, four dully-gleaming, blue-steel beauties.

The tall, lean kid touched each of the guns in turn. His hands were sprinkled with fine golden hairs.

Twice he ran his fingers back and forth over the four guns. Then he picked one of them up. The best one, thought Gabe; he knows his hardware.

The young man hefted the gun in his hand. A long-barrelled Colt forty-four. Built by Gabe to his own particular specifications. A few extra refinements, an hair-trigger among them.

None of the other three guns had such a trigger. The hammer was larger than usual; this was a fast, deadly gunfighter's weapon. Anybody who didn't know how to handle such a gun would run the risk of blowing his own hand off at the twitch of a thumb.

The young man's own thumb, narrow and prehensile, now rested lightly on the hammer. If his approach in the shop, to the bench had been wary and uncertain, there was no uncertainty about him now. He raised his head and met Gabe's eyes with his own pale blue ones, a hint of friendliness in them.

'How much is this one?'

Gabe told him and he took out a large, soiled bundle of notes from inside his belt.

'How many shells?' Gabe showed him the size of the boxes.

'Three I guess.' The young man peeled off the notes.

So much money. And no gun.

A stranger too. Gabe was sure he would have remembered the young man had he seen him before.

Gabe took the notes, gave change.

'Thank you, kindly,' said the young man.

7

He was a Westerner but his accent wasn't easy to place. He certainly wasn't a Texan like Gabe. But, after all, this was Montana. Gabe himself, though he had been in this town six years, was still by way of being a 'foreigner' as far as some folks were concerned.

Most of the natives didn't like strangers. Gabe was certain sure they weren't going to like this one. Gabe watched him as he loaded the gun, slid it into his holster, tucked the rest of the shells into the capacious top pocket of his faded blue shirt.

'Thank you kindly,' he said for the second time.

'My pleasure, suh,' said Gabe.

The young man turned on his heels, began to walk. 'Good day,' he said over his shoulder.

'Good day,' said Gabe. Watching him across the floor, padding soundlessly in his moccasins, blocking out the light momentarily, moving through the door.

… Vanishing from Gabe's sight.

Then the shooting began.

8

TWO

SHOTGUN KILLER

Two shots. Then a whole barrage of them as if a small army had opened up.

Instinctively, Gabe reached for one of the handguns, cursed as he realised they were all empty. A pistol wasn't his style nowadays anyway. He moved along behind the bench. He reached down the double-barrelled shotgun, the only thing in the house that was kept loaded and this only on his wife, Kate's insistence.

He was halfway across the store when his recent customer came backwards through the door, swinging it shut.

'What's the idea?'

At the barked question the young man turned. The blue-steel barrel of the brand-new pistol faced the menacing twin sockets of the old shotgun.

Then the young man lowered his weapon. His eyes were dull and the left shoulder of his shirt was soaked with blood.

'You might need that,' he said, 'if they bust in here after me.'

'Nobody comes in my shop if I don't want them to. Get back there.'

'Be careful.' The young man staggered to the bench then leaned against it.

Gabe's daughter, Prunella, came running into the shop. Her mother Kate was out shopping, but this was a small town and she would have heard the shots.

Eighteen-year-old Prunella halted uncertainly, staring from one to the other of the two men.

'What's the matter?'

Neither of them answered her. The young man leaned against the bench, half-turned towards the girl, his wounded shoulder hidden from her, his gun hanging laxly at the end of his other arm.

Gabe crossed to the window and cautiously looked out. The street was empty, silent, dead. Like a long-forgotten ghost-town preserved miraculously in time.

He came away from the window.

'Stay where you are, Prunella,' he said gently.

The young stranger turned completely around then and got a good look at the girl. Gabe recognised the impact her beauty had upon him. He had seen the same sort of reaction on men many times over the last couple of years. Then it was as if the stranger lost all control over his limbs. The gun clattered to the floor. The man slumped forward across the bench.

'Father – he's hurt!' cried the girl.

'I can handle him. Get back in there.' Gabe's tone was harsher than he had intended it to be.

He saw the hurt flare in the girl's eyes. Then she turned and disappeared through the curtains into the back place.

The stranger moaned as Gabe reached him. 'Try and help yourself, son.' Gabe picked up the gun, tucked it into the belt beneath his white apron. He got the young man's arm over his own broad, now-stooping shoulders, held on to the shot-

10

gun with his other hand, thinking wryly that he might need it yet.

They stumbled through into the back place. Prunella took one good look at the young stranger, said, 'I'll get some hot water,' and disappeared into the kitchen.

'Good girl,' Gabe called after her, trying to make up for his earlier roughness.

He helped the stranger onto the battered couch, laid him flat with two cushions behind his head.

Gabe was worried about Kate, his wife. If she, having heard the shooting, came racing back here and those hardcases, whoever they were, were waiting....

He turned towards the young man again, opened his mouth to say something, closed it again. The patient was unconscious. Laying him flat had helped to stop the flow of blood from the shoulder, however.

Gabe took up the shotgun and went back into the shop again, moving very swiftly for so large a man, bulky now from too much semi-sedentary work. The West was a young man's country and he was young no longer. For a moment he wished he was that kid back there, bullet in shoulder or no bullet in shoulder.

The street brooded silently. Empty.

Gabe retraced his steps. The wounded visitor was still unconscious, his moccasined feet dangling from the end of the couch. Gabe went on through to the kitchen. Prunella was pouring boiling water into a bowl.

'Anybody lurking out back?'

'I haven't seen anybody. What's this all about, Dad?'

He told her what had happened. But the identity of the moccasined young stranger and the reason for the shooting was as much a mystery to him as it was to her.

He peeped through the kitchen window. The yard was

11

empty of everything except litter and he made a mental note to give the place a good going over as soon as possible.

The only thing out there that could conceal a man was the privy. And there was only room to hide one man inside or outside of this. The door was shut. Beyond the privy was the open range, scrubby and flat, with stunted trees in the distance. Hardly room for a prairie-dog to hide, unless he stayed in his hole in the ground.

This town, Benton City, was, despite the grandiose title, little more than one long main street of rutted ground and sagging boardwalk. Small tributaries were springing out from it here and there. But here at the end of the street the back of Gabe Parker's gunsmith's shop looked out upon desolation.

A gambler named Jules Benton, from the Barbary Coast, had started the town and given it its name. In those days – and they weren't so very long ago – Benton City had been 'wide open' in every sense of this time-honoured Western phase.

The clapboard saloons, the tent-casinos and brothels had boomed for twenty-four hours daylight and dark. The gamblers, the girls, the peddlers, the roustabouts had worked in shifts.

Benton City had no law but the cynical one of Jules Benton and his hardcases. Human vultures, human wolves, human jackals and coyotes.

But, like vultures squabbling over a carcass they finished up by fighting among themselves, by fouling their own nests.

Jules Benton was already middle-aged and in ill-health when he spawned his original clapboard and tent town. He died suddenly, choking on his own bile after a gargantuan drinking bout. And rivals moved in and his lieutenants squabbled among themselves, grabbing for an uneasy crown.

People still remembered the holocaust that ensued and the way that the law, of a fashion, came to Benton City.

They had a marshal now, a bovine elderly man named Pete Bickerston.

Rather by process of circumstances than by any undue effort on the part of Marshal Bickerston, Benton City was now a peaceable backwater.

It lived upon itself and upon the small ranchers and farmers who had settled in the area within five or ten miles of the town and where the pastureland was richer if not actually lush.

The town had even become dull, pompous, hypocritical, attempting to eradicate all memories of the 'roaring days'. It had become rather prissy, like an elderly ex-madam turned respectable.

The wild boys had moved to richer stamping grounds. They only passed through from time to time while the townsfolk held their breath, waited, hoped, prayed a little in their leaning clapboard chapel.

Old Pete Bickerston stayed in his office with a bottle and hoped he would not be called upon to enforce the law he represented. Everybody waited, walked warily and sang small until the wild boys had left again, as they always did, for organised vice was non-existent here now, the area was comparatively poor, the pickings slender.

So this was Benton City after Gabe Parker had been settled there for six years. Even he remembered the old days – not so old really – and he hadn't done so badly then, for the wild boys respected his creative skill and recommended him widely. Many of them still called on him, purely for business reasons, when they were 'passing through'.

Gabe was a big fellow with a quite forthright way with him. He gave the appearance of fearing no man; and loving

13

no man, only his guns and his family. And the wild boys respected him for this too: they certainly did not despise him and harry him as they did the other shopkeepers of the town.

The six years of the semi-sedentary life had taken its toll of Gabe. He was heavier now and a little stooped. His darkly handsome face was fleshier around the chin and furrowed at cheek and brow. His black hair was shot with wings of grey and he had it cropped much shorter than he used to in the old days.

The old days were gone; he was getting old too. The past was the past and he was contented and at peace here with his wife and his daughter and his few good friends.

And if he ever itched a little for the old days the feeling soon passed.

But now his little peaceful world seemed to have blown up in his face.

And strangely enough, though momentarily he might have been off-balance, he was off-balance no longer. And it was as if the long, peaceful days and the years had never been.

Prunella started to carry the steaming bowl of water into the other room. Gabe checked her with a touch of his free hand.

'Let me go first,' he said.

He held the shotgun in a firing position in front of him. And it was well that he did. When he got through the communicating door, the second stranger was standing just inside the curtain at the other side of the room. He must have entered the shop silently and come right through.

He was big and dark and badly needed a shave. His gun was out and pointed at the unconscious form on the couch.

The gun-muzzle was lifted now as the man's gaze changed. Gabe saw the savagery flare in the dark eyes.

14

The old killer look. The hammer cocked, the finger tightening.

Hesitation meant death. Gabe fired one barrel of the shotgun.

The terrible blast of the shell was deafening in the enclosed place. The man was knocked backwards. As if he had been taken by a sudden gush of wind, a storm of violence.

He screamed once, horribly, as he disappeared through the curtains, leaving them flapping wildly behind him.

But they fell softly and soon became still. And, after the storm and the savagery, there was utter silence.

The years had rolled back and Gabe Parker had felt the old killing urge, the naked exultation.

And he had killed. As he had had to.

It had been him or the other one. His life – and the life of the young man on the couch perhaps, and the life of his daughter Prunella – against that of the unshaven visitor, a lobo wolf if Gabe had ever seen one.

He had killed. Justifiably, if not too cleanly. He had always hated shotguns....

Justice was on his side. But still he felt suddenly sick to his stomach. And tired. And older than he had ever felt in his life before.

THREE

BATTLE IN THE STREET

Prunella came through the door. She was pale, but she looked steady enough. Gabe was glad she could not see the man on the other side of the curtains.

Mechanically, she placed the steaming bowl of water on a nearby table.

Gabe crossed to her, handed her the shotgun.

'You know how to use this.'

It was a statement rather than a question. She nodded, her lips compressed.

'Watch the back. If anybody tries to get in, shoot 'em.'

She nodded again. Gabe's heart swelled with pride. His tired feeling left him. He realized he had acted in all this with instinctive decisiveness. And his daughter, a spunky girl, was taking her pattern from him.

He took the Colt .44 from beneath his apron. The hair-trigger pistol that the young stranger had bought, had taken, and, in an unorthodox fashion, had returned.

Gabe spun the barrel. Only one shot had been fired.

He crossed to the curtains that separated the shop from the living-room. With a sweep of his arms he signalled to Prunella to get out of the line of fire.

He heard her move.

He moved to one side of the curtains and reached out a long arm and pulled them slowly apart. Nothing happened. He went through.

The body lay at his feet and the shop was empty, the door shut.

The silence was absolute again. None of the cheerful sounds that were usually heard from the street at this time of morning. Steeling himself, Gabe looked down at the hulk at his feet. A man with his throat and chest blown away was not pretty.

Gabe hadn't thought he had the stomach for this sort of thing any more.

He was surprised to find himself unmoved by the sight, ice-cold.

He strode over the body and moved across the shop, calling over his shoulder as he did so, 'You all right Prunella?'

'Yes.' The reply came clearly from behind him.

He reached the window, peered cautiously out. His heart almost stopped at what he saw.

His ice-cold decisiveness left him. He began to tremble.

His wife Kate was crossing the street at a half-trot. There was an anxious look on her lined, handsome face beneath the beautiful cloud of prematurely-white hair.

The West was hard on a woman. But Kate was born and bred on the frontier and had never wanted another life.

She was completely fearless. Even foolhardy.

She was being foolhardy now. She had heard the shots.

Like a mountain-lion defending its young – and she treated both Gabe and her daughter like children sometimes – she was running to the rescue without consideration of danger.

A man, a stranger, ran across from behind Kate. Gabe opened the door of the store and stepped out.

Kate half-turned as the man approached her. She saw the gun he held. As Gabe saw it too, raised his own.

Kate lifted the loaded canvas shopping-bag she carried. As if she would use it as a sort of club-like sling. But the man menaced her with the gun: Gabe saw his lips move but could not hear what he said. And even Kate was not foolhardy enough to argue with a loaded gun, a threat of death. She lowered the bag. She was directly in the line of fire between Gabe and the stranger.

The stranger grabbed her arm. 'We're coming over, old-timer,' he yelled. 'Drop the gun or I shoot the lady.'

Gabe let the gun fall. It hit the boardwalk with a loud clatter, mocking him. He stood motionless, his broad shoulders stooped, his arms hanging impotently.

The gunman held on to Kate's arm with his free hand. He shepherded her forward while his gun pointed straight at the unarmed Gabe.

Gabe could see that his wife was beside herself with rage, but she was having to do as she was told. And Gabe himself was ice cold again, a man waiting for a chance.

The gunman turned his head a little but not enough to enable Kate or her husband to try anything. They all heard the footsteps then; thumping slowly on the boardwalk.

Gabe Parker was surprised to see Marshal Pete Bickerston coming down the main street. Gun in hand, he was moving along the boardwalk in an attempt to outflank the gunman.

Here and there a townsman lurked in the background. Having raked the law out to investigate the shooting they were now prepared to let the law take its course.

The poor fool, thought Gabe. The poor godforsaken old soak.

He watched, powerless yet. But he tensed himself, waited his chance.

'Get back, old man,' shouted the gunman. 'Or I'll shoot the woman.'

He was getting savage. The savagery was in the hoarseness of his voice. *Please do as he says, Pete.* Gabe Parker did not speak the words aloud; they vibrated through him like a prayer.

But Marshal Pete Bickerston had come too far to turn back now.

He had been a good lawman in his younger days. Not a notoriously fast gun. But steady. He had outlived many of the faster ones.

Maybe a spark of the old courage had goaded him this time. Or maybe it was just the effects of recently-imbibed hooch.

He halted now but he did not turn.

Gabe Parker thought, if that snake shoots Kate he'll have two guns – mine and Pete's – to contend with: we'd have him in a crossfire. But, good God above, that wouldn't help dear Kate at all. Gabe hoped and prayed that the gunman wouldn't lose his head, thumb the hammer of the gun he had pointed at Kate's back.

'Let Mrs Parker go,' shouted Pete Bickerston. 'Throw down your gun, son – I'm takin' you in.'

Even from where he stood outside his shop, Gabe Parker could hear the tremble in the old lawman's voice. While he admired the old man's new-found courage, he cursed him for his foolhardiness. Pete should know you couldn't waste time bandying words with a lobo wolf like that one. Old age or liquor, or both, seemed to have impaired Pete's judgement. Kate's life hung in the balance.

Everything hung in the balance. For a nerve-wracking palpitating moment of time.

Gabe Parker, unarmed, big hands hanging, his gun at his feet on the boardwalk before the gunsmith's. The gunman and the woman, caught, immobile in the centre of the baked, cart-rutted streets under the hard glare of the sun. Caught in that moment of time.

And the old man on the other boardwalk, a floppy-looking figure like a badly-stuffed scarecrow. The sun glinting on his star, his badge of office that – in this moment of time – was no longer the mockery it had so recently been. And his old long-barrelled Frontier Colt levelled steadily.

Even if he *had* been drinking, it didn't seem to be affecting his gun hand.

And it was he who once more became the decisive one.

He began to move along the boardwalk, again.

The gunman swung around and fired, the report almost simultaneous with the movement. Pete Bickerston jerked as if he had been struck by an invisible fist. His gun pitched from his hand, fell in the dust. He hit a hitching-post with his broad back and it held him up.

But Kate Parker was acting too. In that split second in which the fast-shooting killer's attention was deflected from her, she swung her shopping bag.

It caught the man a tremendous buffet on his shoulder and he staggered. Kate threw herself down in the dusty street. With near incredible speed for so heavy a man Gabe Parker scooped up the gun from his feet; he dropped to one knee as he levelled, fired. Two shots. So close together that the reports made one rolling, echoing sound.

The gunman was fast too. But not fast enough this time:

Kate's desperate action had given her husband his chance. The gunman's slug merely smashed a window in the upper storey of the gunsmith's.

The man was spun like a top by Gabe's shots. Both of them found their target. In the chest, in the shoulder.

The man hit the dust belly down. He flopped a couple of times, then became still. His gun lay a few inches away from his motionless clawed fingers.

Gabe Parker jerked to his feet. He whirled instinctively as he heard footsteps behind him. His lips were drawn back from his teeth.

But he slumped then. It was Prunella with the shotgun.

'God,' he said hoarsely. 'I almost shot you.'

'Are you all right, Dad?'

'Yes. You?'

'Yes. Nobody's bothered me. The young man's still unconscious.'

She looked past him. Her mother, regaining her feet, was running across to Pete Bickerston who still sagged against the hitching-post, both hands clasped across his paunch.

'I think there were only two of them,' said Gabe.

'I'll go back in,' Prunella said and turned.

Gabe hesitated a moment then followed her through the shop. He strode over the body of the first gunman. Prunella kept her head high.

The young stranger still lay supine on the couch in the living-room. He was too long for this improvised bed and his moccasined feet looked slightly grotesque.

The blood was drying in an ugly brown patch at his shoulder.

'I'll bathe that wound,' said Prunella matter-of-factly. 'But I shall have to heat some more water first.'

Gabe followed her into the kitchen, took another look

21

outside. Nothing more. All was silent again.

'Keep the shotgun handy, *chiquita*,' he said. 'I'll go see what can be done for old Pete.'

'Poor Mr Bickerston,' said Prunella softly.

'Maybe it isn't as bad as it looks,' said Gabe reassuringly.

He went back and out into the street. He stepped around the second body; the flies were already gathering in a buzzing cloud in the sunlight. He crossed to the little knot of people on the opposite boardwalk. Pete Bickerston at their centre, laid flat now, a coat beneath his head, Kate kneeling beside him.

Gabe elbowed his way through, not troubling to disguise the contempt he felt for these folks who had lurked in the background while the old man got himself shot.

Kate looked up. 'He's still alive, Gabe. But he's in a bad way.'

Her gaze raked the faces of the onlookers. 'Two of you get him into his place.' Her voice lashed them like a whip.

Then Kate's voice changed again. 'Is Prunella all right, Gabe?'

'Yes, she's fine.'

'You better stay with her, huh. I'll do what I can for Pete.'

'All right, Kate.'

Gabe watched two of the townsmen carry the unconscious marshal, his hands still folded over his bloodstained middle, in the direction of his office.

Kate bustled in the rear. She would take care of things all right at that end. She was a staunch frontierswoman. Death and violence were not new to her. She had a way with bullet wounds. Gabe hoped she could work some kind of miracle on Pete Bickerston.

FOUR

THE EXPERT

By now a group of townsfolk had gathered round the body in the street. They turned their heads as, on his way back to the store, Gabe approached them.

Their faces mirrored various emotions. But the main one, even with those of them who knew Gabe best, was one of a sort of wariness. This was a new Gabe to them. A Gabe who, though they admired his skill as a gunsmith, they had not expected to act like another kind of gun-expert too. Gabe as a gunfighter. Gabe who had just killed a man. Swiftly, terribly, cleanly. Killed him as instantly and as irrevocably dead as any man can be.

Gabe put his foot beneath the body and rolled it over so that the face was revealed.

'Anybody know him?'

They all shook their heads.

Big Lon Staflen, the walrus-moustached blacksmith, had just arrived, come late on the scene. As far as Gabe Parker was concerned, Big Lon was the most likeable man in town. They were good friends, he and Lon.

The blacksmith's shop was at the other end of town. Gabe knew that if Lon could have got here sooner, he wouldn't have lurked in the background. He would have been right there with Marshal Bickerston, taking a hand.

He still carried his heavy hammer. He looked disgruntled at his own tardiness. He said:

'Nasty-looking gent. You ever seen him before, Gabe?'

'Can't say I have.'

'Was he after you?'

'No.'

Gabe told them about the young man lying wounded in the back room, about the other dead man in the shop. The two gunmen must have been lying in wait for the young stranger. They had almost got him.

Gabe hadn't seen any of them before, the two dead ones, the young wounded one. He didn't know what the quarrel was about. The wounded one hadn't been able to talk yet. Maybe he had regained consciousness by now.

Gabe didn't think there had been more than two gunmen chasing the younker with the moccasins. But he couldn't be sure and he was anxious about Prunella back there in the shop with the wounded man. He wasted no more time in talking but made a beeline for his door. The knot of townsfolk followed him.

They followed him into the dusky interior of the store. Like children fascinated by the forbidden, they clustered to inspect the second body.

None of them were strangers to violence and death. But their recent peaceable days had softened their shells. Had softened their innards too, thought Gabe Parker savagely, if their lack of action in backing up Pete Bickerston was anything to go by.

The second body was a nasty sight. The man's features

were still fairly distinct, however. But none of the townsfolk had ever seen him before.

'He's in the way here, Gabe,' said Big Lon Staflen unemotionally. 'Shall I shift him?'

'Please, Lon.'

The big walrus-moustached man leaned his hammer against Gabe's gun-bench. He got hold of the dead man's feet and dragged him away from the curtains. He laid him against the wall, hidden by a row of barrels in which Gabe kept guncotton and sawdust and oddments.

'Could we take a look at the wounded man, Gabe?' said Ed Cranthorpe, mayor of Benton City.

Ed was a lawyer, a fat little man with a pompous voice and manner. But he had a kind heart and was always glad to put his legal knowledge to the use of the underdog. He could be forthright when need be. His mayoralty was merely a token position, but Ed enjoyed it. And if the town needed a mayor at all, Ed Cranthorpe was the obvious choice. Ed had big ideas for Benton City.

Gabe Parker wondered where Ed had been while the battle raged. He said: 'It's no use all of us trooping in there. You, Ed, and Big Lon come in with me. The rest of you stay here.'

Put in their places, the rest of the little bunch shuffled their feet and said nothing.

'Lead the way then, Gabe,' said the mayor. He and Big Lon followed the gunsmith through the curtains into the living-room.

The young stranger was conscious. He was even sitting up. His leg were still on the couch, the moccasined feet sticking out.

Prunella was standing at the table, wringing out a bloodstained cloth into the bowl.

The stranger was watching her as if her dark beauty, or his weakness, or both, had him mesmerised. His face was white. Pain had tautened its lines, making him look older.

Prunella nodded at her father and the two other men but did not say anything right away. Her movements were quick and efficient.

She wasn't merely decorative. She knew what she was doing too. Her whole manner implied that this was women's work. Nurse's work. She had to see to her patient first. These other men would await her pleasure.

She carried the bowl into the kitchen. She returned almost immediately with fresh hot water.

'How're you feeling, son?' asked Gabe.

'Not so bad, thank you kindly,' said the young man. His shirt had been cut neatly down the side. He held a pad of clean white cloth to his shoulder, but took it away quickly now as Prunella approached him with another one, hot and steaming.

'Lean back,' she said.

Meekly, the young man did as he was told.

He winced as the hot compress was placed on the ugly wound.

'His name's George,' said the girl to nobody in particular. 'That much I've been able to get from him so far. He's got a bullet in that shoulder and it'll have to come out. You better get your scalpel, Dad.'

Years ago Gabe had taken a set of surgeon's implements from a doctor in payment of a debt. He had become quite proficient with them; though he hadn't used them for some time, particularly on anything as serious as a bullet-wound.

He fetched the small, oblong well-worn case from a cupboard in the kitchen, placed it on the living-room table, lifted the lid. The instruments gleamed cheerfully up at him. Almost as pretty a sight as a pair of matched, silver-tooled derringers.

He selected his favourite scalpel, the narrow, wicked-looking one that had been used as a probe on more than a few occasions in the old days.

'Get the whiskey, Prunella,' he said. He was taking charge now.

His daughter hastened to do his bidding. She gave him the whiskey, a full bottle. He handed the scalpel to her to be scalded. He took the cork out of the bottle and handed the whiskey to the young man called George.

'Take a good slug, son. As much as you can manage.'

George grinned, his taut pain-wracked face becoming boyish again beneath its thatch of blond hair. He lifted the bottle to his lips. Judging then by his performance, George could manage quite a lot.

Big Lon Staflen took the bottle. Gabe Parker got to work with the scalpel. The bullet was deep. Great globules of sweat stood on the young man's face but he made no sound.

'There's the little beggar,' said Gabe finally. 'Take another drink, son. I guess you need it.'

Again George did as he was told. Big Lon and Mayor Ed Cranthorpe watched with fascination as the level of the liquid in the bottle went slowly but surely down.

But finally young George had had what he needed and Gabe said, 'Pour one for Ed and yourself, Lon,' and Prunella was there ready with glasses, smiling mischievously at the two men.

Uncle Ed and Uncle Lon she always called them. She had been only ten when her parents first arrived in Benton City. Lon and his wife, Sue, and Ed and his wife, Ruby – dead now these two years – had been the Parker family's earliest friends.

Lon and Ed grinned at each other. Mayor Ed's official-type pomposity fell from him like a cloak when he was in the company of his best friends, the folks who knew him and took delight in joshing him about his little foibles. He enjoyed their joshing. He and Ed and Gabe killed the rest of the bottle while Prunella bound up the young stranger's shoulder.

George dozed off to sleep.

'It's a wonder all that hooch he took didn't knock him plumb flat out right off,' Big Lon commented.

'Leave him be,' said Prunella with mock severity.

Chuckling, her father and the two other men left the living-room. They became grave again as they faced the other townsfolk, still waiting in the shop.

'Pity that younker didn't talk some before he went to sleep,' said Ed. 'I hope there aren't any more gunfighters lurking around.'

That, indeed, was a sobering thought.

FIVE

THE RUNAWAY

Two more individuals appeared in the doorway of the shop. A grotesque-looking pair. But turning towards them as one man, the townsfolk showed no surprise. They were accustomed to seeing these two together.

The townsfolk awaited with interest, however, the reactions of these newcomers.

The enormous one in the checked red shirt which made him look like some grotesque balloon was, of all things, the town's one and only undertaker.

His name was Grif Kallis. Although his form and garb didn't fit the popular conception of a Western undertaker – black and lean like a lugubrious gambler – his face did. It wasn't as big as one would have expected it to be. It perched on top of Grif's enormous frame like a boil on a fat squaw.

There was plenty of chin and neck. But then the face sloped upwards almost into the shape of a pear on which Grif's battered brown derby was balanced at a precarious angle. And Grif's face, with its tiny eyes, button nose and wide, curved-down mouth looked as if it was about to disintegrate into tears at any moment. It always looked like that. Grif Kallis had never been known to smile.

By contrast his companion was a crippled gnome of a man. Barnaby Jimson, the livery man, had far more to weep about than his bosom friend, Grif. But Barnaby was the one who always smiled. He hopped forward now, his club-foot thumping the boards.

'Where's the other one?' he carolled in the magpie voice. 'Let my friend, Grif, measure him up.'

'Over here,' said Big Lon Staflen, jerking his bullet head.

Barnaby hopped over to the body behind the barrels. Grif brought up the wake in a stately manner.

'Ooh, messy,' said Barnaby. 'Ain't he messy, Grif?'

Grif nodded his head slowly and mournfully. 'Have you seen him before, Barney?' he asked. His voice was like the tolling of a funeral bell.

'Nope.' Barnaby shook his head, his eyes dancing like a mischievous starling's. 'Nope.'

'Have you seen the other one before either, Barney?' asked Mayor Ed Cranthorpe with a jerk of his thumb in the direction of the street.

If anybody had seen these strangers before, Barnaby Jimson had, for he owned the only livery-stable in town, next door to his friend, Grif's undertaking parlour. Barnaby always said that if somebody fell off a horse outside his stable and broke his neck, they wouldn't have far to drag the body. This hadn't happened yet, but, folks said, big fat Grif was still hoping. No wonder he was so enormous: he was surely the laziest cuss alive.

He was wheezing and sweating now as he bent over the mutilated body of the shotgun victim, eyeing it with professional interest, measuring it for size. It was second nature for him to do this; though, if somebody didn't cough up the necessary for a plain box this body and the one outside would be wrapped in sackcloth and dropped in an unnamed hole on Boot Hill.

Barnaby Jimson, answering the mayor's question, said he hadn't seen either of the two dead men before.

'Have you seen any strangers at all ride into town today?' asked Gabe Parker.

Barnaby looked at Gabe. 'Ah, my gunfighter friend!' he crowed. He could be malicious at times. But now his wide grin took the sting out of his words.

He went on: 'There was one stranger this mornin' – left his horse at my place. Young feller with yaller hair. Rode in on a little palomino. No saddle. Just a horse-blanket. Home-made rope stirrups too. Just like an Injun. Come to think of it, he wore moccasins like an Injun, too. But he was no Injun, not with that yaller hair. Politely spoken young cuss too.'

'The young man in the other room,' said Mayor Cranthorpe explosively in his plump little turkey-cock way.

Barnaby jerked his head on one side like an inquisitive bird. 'Come again?'

'He's in my living-room on the couch, that yellow-haired boy,' explained Gabe Parker. 'It was him those two gunslingers were after. One of 'em got him in the shoulder.'

'Didn't do 'em much good though did it, Gabe, thanks to you?' Barnaby Jimson's monkey grin was wider than ever. 'I'd like to say howdy to that young feller again.'

'Come on then,' said Gabe, brusquely, and led the way through the curtain.

He stopped dead on the threshold of the living-room. Barnaby crowded at his heels, hopping from side to side, trying to see past Gabe's bulk.

The couch was empty.

The room was empty.

31

Moving very swiftly Gabe went through to the kitchen. That was empty too.

He turned, almost running into Barnaby.

The door to the stairs opened and Prunella stood there. Her gaze went to the couch.

'Dad – where is he?'

'That's what I'd like to know.'

'He was there on the couch when I went upstairs – about five minutes ago. He looked as if he was still asleep.'

'Hey,' said Barnaby. 'Looks like he left a note.'

He picked up a folded sheet of grimy paper from the cushions of the couch.

Gabe took it from him, unfolded it.

The message bore no salutation. It had been scrawled hurriedly with a badly-sharpened pencil.

Thank you. For me to stay might endanger family. So long.

Wordlessly, Gabe passed the message to his daughter.

She read it. 'He must have slipped out the back way,' she said. 'He shouldn't be moving so soon, not with that shoulder.'

Gabe turned to Barnaby. 'Let's get down to the livery stable.'

He had killed two men today. It had been him or them. But still he wanted to know why this had had to be. And the yellow-haired, moccassined youngster called George was, as far as Gabe knew, the only one who could answer his questions.

So that they wouldn't have to waste time explaining things to the townsfolk outside, Gabe and Barnaby used the back way to the stables, the route that the yellow-haired George must have used before them.

'Don't wait for me,' said Barnaby.

Considering his small stature and his disability, the livery-

32

man could move remarkably fast. But he couldn't possibly keep up with Gabe, who forged ahead.

As he approached the back of the stable, the gunsmith realised he hadn't thought to bring a weapon with him. Which was a bit thoughtless, considering the wording of George's note.

But it was too late to turn back now.

Gabe moved cautiously through the back door of the stables and into the sunshot gloom. A horse nickered softly. Another pawed the ground.

Gabe halted, stood still in the shadows beside the door, got his eyes accustomed to the sun-dappled shadows.

There was no human person there, only horses. And no palomino, at that. There had been no saddle, Barnaby had said, just a blanket. How long did it take a man to throw a blanket across a horse's back?

The yellow-haired George with his palomino and his blanket and his rope stirrups – the whole caboodle, such as it was – why, they were probably a mile or so away by now.

And, unless he had stolen a gun from somewhere during his flight, the crazy young fool was unarmed.

But wait a minute! Gabe himself had carried George's pistol in his belt for a bit. He had killed the second gunman with it. Then afterwards while he was talking to the mayor and Big Lon he had put it on the table in the living-room. Maybe George had picked it up.

If the contents of George's note weren't just a sort of white lie, an alibi for him leaving so soon, there was plenty of reason for Gabe to suppose that the young man badly needed a gun. For if, as George had implied, his benefactor and his benefactor's family would be in danger if he stuck around, there must have been more than just two hardcases on his trail.

Those two hadn't looked like lawmen, so that theory was ruled out. so why was George on the run? Who wanted him and why? He had revealed a sizeable wad of notes when he paid Gabe for the pistol. But there hadn't been enough there to warrant his being chased across the countryside by a bunch of hardcases out for his blood.

Gabe's mind raced. His feet moved onwards. Then he was out the other side of the stable and in main street. But, of course, there was still no sign of the palomino and his yellow-haired rider.

Gabe retraced his steps. Barnaby joined him in the stable. They walked back along the cluttered, dusty rear of the main street.

Gabe questioned Barnaby. But Barnaby couldn't remember the yellow-haired kid saying anything of interest, anything about himself, his past, his ultimate destination.

'I figured him for a drifter,' said Barnaby.

They got back to the shop. There was no gun on the living-room table.

The townsfolk had moved back into the street, were drifting away. Grif Kallis and the one-eyed boy who was his helper had taken the two bodies away in the undertaker's cart.

Big Lon Staflen and the mayor still waited, were surprised to hear that the wounded man had taken a *pasear* and it didn't appear he was coming back. But there was nothing they could do about it. They said So-long, said they'd see Gabe in the saloon that evening. They went away and Barnaby Jimson said So-long, too, and limped after them.

Gabe would have liked to go and see how Marshal Bickerston was faring. But he didn't like to leave Prunella on her own. He'd have to go into the front and wait until Kate came in with the news.

Prunella came down the stairs, saying her chores were

34

finished. She knew that her father and Barnaby hadn't caught up with the wounded man.

'Shall I make some coffee, Dad?'

'Please do, *chiquita*.'

She made for the kitchen, paused at the communicating door, turned.

'I put the gun back in the shop, on the bench. I emptied the shells out first.'

'What gun?'

'The new gun. The one with the hair-trigger. The one you used. It was on the table.' She pointed.

'Oh,' said Gabe 'All right, Pru. Thanks.'

He did not speak what else was in his mind.

Prunella disappeared in the kitchen.

So he didn't take his gun with him after all, reflected Gabe. Probably he was in such a hurry to get out that he didn't spot it there on the table. Still....

Gabe had had him figured for a gunfighter. Young – but with all the signs.

But the young fool hadn't acted like a gunfighter this time.

Had he been too hasty because he was badly frightened?

Or because, as he had implied in his note, he was anxious not to bring grief to other people?

Maybe it had been a bit of both....

SIX

MAN AT THE DOOR

Kate returned. Her classical, young-looking face beneath the cloud of white hair wore an anxious frown.

'Pete's still alive,' she said. 'But he's bad. I'm worried about him. Doc Craven's with him now.'

Gabe told her how everything had happened. He was sorry she hadn't got to see the young man called George.

Maybe she would see him after all. Maybe they both would see him again. Though he didn't say so, Gabe hoped that if and when they saw the young George again it would be under favourable circumstances – not thrown face downwards over a horse's back like a badly-filled sack of meal.

Gabe – and Kate – had seen too many young men finish that way. Gabe had almost finished that way himself on more than one occasion.

And if young George was *unarmed*.... And with that shoulder....

'Will you be all right if I go down and see Pete?'

'Why wouldn't I be all right?'

'Well, like I said, there may be others apart from those two.

36

I....' Gabe let his sentence tail off.

'I've got the shotgun,' said Kate soberly. 'I'd use it too, you know that.'

It was her way of reassuring him.

'Don't you know that?' she asked.

'I know that,' he said.,

'Take a gun with you.'

'All right.'

He took the hair-trigger Colt .44. The one he had used before. The one that by rights belonged to young George, the kid with the yellow hair and moccasins, the kid with the busted shoulder....

Why did he keep thinking about that kid? Because of that kid two men had been killed.

The kid was a danger. Gabe's peaceful life – the life he had built for himself over these six years – was broken because of him.

Gabe didn't want his family – young Prunella particularly – anywhere near a kid like that one.

It was a good job young George had run out like he had. In that he'd had sense – of a sort. He was gone! Most probably he was gone for good and all. So there was no sense in anybody in Benton City wondering and worrying about him anymore....

People looked at him, Gabe Parker, as he walked along the street. Still in his grimy white apron. Bareheaded, without a coat. A gun in his belt. Hidden by his apron. Here nobody could see it.

But it might just as well be out in the open – with a gunbelt and holster too maybe – right out where everybody could see it. Strapped to his waist. Tied down with a whang string maybe. The way the Kid George's had been. Though that holster had been empty. Was it still empty? Or had George...?

Drat that kid!

Yes, people looked at Gabe Parker as, bareheaded in the sunshine, he walked along main street of Benton City. Some of them spoke to him. But they looked at him in a different way.

This was the Gabe Parker who had killed two men. It was all over town by now. People were on their way to the gunsmith's to take a look at the scene of the shooting. The disgruntled latecomers getting a vicarious thrill. They stared at Gabe. They spoke softly among themselves. Here was a gunsmith who knew more about guns than anybody had suspected.

He was one of the old ones. Before the time of some of them. Even six or seven years was 'way back' to them. He was one from the old 'bloody' days.

Like the old marshal, Pete Bickerston, who was dying 'twas said. Like Big Lon Staflen, the blacksmith. Like Grif Kallis, the enormous undertaker who had such a creepy way with him. And Grif's friend, the little club-footed Barnaby Jimson. Like the mayor even; plump, pompous, kindly, Ed Cranthorpe. Like old Doc Craven who had dug out so many bullets in the old days, or had stood impotently and watched men die.

Doc Craven who turned to face Gabe Parker now as Gabe entered the marshal's office. Doc, six-foot and over, and with an emaciation that made him look even taller, despite his stoop. With his grey hair worn long, waving almost to his shoulders the way some of the old timers still wore it. With his narrow, pale, lantern-jawed face and the glitter of his blue eyes and his arrogant manner which antagonised people who didn't know him.

But Gabe Parker knew him well, was fond of him, respected him.

Doc had been washing his hands at the little sink. He jerked his leonine head.

'He's in there.'

'How is he?'

'Not good. I've taken the slug out and made him comfortable. I've done all I can for the time being. The rest is up to him. He's still a tough old buzzard. But you know how he's been living these last few years.'

Gabe nodded. The booze! Yes, the booze might kill Pete yet. Still, if he got over this – and he'd have his self-respect back right enough – maybe he'd leave the booze alone and live to a ripe old age.

Gabe moved toward the middle door. He paused when Doc called his name.

'You did a good job out there.'

'I'm not particularly proud of it, Doc. But I wished I could've been quicker, saved Pete from that.'

Doc shrugged into his rusty black coat, made no further comment.

At first Gabe thought Pete was dead. His plump face seemed to have collapsed; it looked like a ghastly white death's head.

He was asleep. Gabe heard his breathing and didn't like the sound of it. But, no more than Doc Craven, there was nothing he could do.

He was disappointed that he hadn't been able to speak to the marshal. But what would he have said? What *could* he have said?

Pete had done what he had had to do. Gabe had done what he had had to do. Kate had helped too. It could be Kate lying near to death. Or Gabe himself. But it was neither of them, it was Pete. And Pete was the law, so maybe it was fitting that he should be the one.

Gabe rejoined Doc Craven, who said he would send a nurse to stay with Pete.

They walked down the street together and Gabe left Doc at the saloon over which he had his rooms, though he did not himself drink anything stronger than sarsparilla, thus refuting the legend that all Western sawbones were drunks.

He didn't pack a gun either, he was no Doc Holliday. Neither was he an Easterner who had failed back there and had come West to bury himself among the obscure and forgotten. He was a Westerner and proud of it. He had learned his profession here in a hard and bloody school. He had never wanted to be anywhere else.

After leaving Doc, Gabe Parker continued homewards.

Kate met him in the shop.

'There's a man been to see you. A stranger.'

'Another stranger?'

'Well, I'd never seen him before. Youngish – but no kid anymore. Lean and tall. Very dark. Black hair, worn long, almost as long as Doc Craven's. Jet black, very thick, like rope. Peculiar thing about it though. Had a broad streak of silver right over the middle. Like this.' Kate ran her finger over the top of her own premature-white hair.

She went on: 'He came to the kitchen door. I met him with the shotgun. I wasn't taking any chances.'

'Did he have anybody with him?'

'Didn't see anybody. Only his horse. He'd left it out by the privy. He was polite, held his hat in his hand while he talked to me. That's how come I noticed that streak o' silver in his hair – couldn't miss it. He asked if Mr Parker was at home and I said No and he asked where were you? I told him it was none of his business. I asked him who he was and what he wanted. He got cagey then. He just said to tell you an old friend had

40

called, then he went. I watched him ride away; way out until he disappeared. I didn't see anybody else.'

'What did you make of him, Kate?'

'I didn't like the look of him at all. A gunslinger. One of the worst kind. The fancy kind. Like a dressed-up rattlesnake. Poisonous.... Mean anything to you, Gabe?'

Gabe shook his head slowly from side to side. 'What did he talk like?'

'Talked fancy too. Could be a Texan though. Down from on the border someplace anyway, I'd say. He's a long way from home....'

Kate paused. Then she asked softly, 'Could it be somebody from the old days, Gabe?'

'I don't know, Kate. I don't remember anybody answering to that description. Time passes though. People change. He'll come back I suppose, whoever he is.'

'I hope he doesn't come back,' said Kate vehemently. And then with a characteristic gesture, a sideways chop of her hand, she dismissed the stranger.

'How's old Pete?' she asked.

'Not good. He was sleeping. He looked awful. Doc doesn't seem very optimistic about him. He implied that it was part-ways up to Pete himself now – if Pete'll fight.'

'He hasn't done any fighting in years until this morning,' said Kate. 'Maybe he'll keep on fighting now.'

'I hope he does. He certainly showed folks here something this morning.'

'So did you, Gabe. So did you.' Kate led the way into the living-room, where Prunella was beginning to prepare the midday meal.

Gabe went into the back to wash. He wasn't very hungry.

There was still blood to wash away out there in the shop.

He wished this morning had never happened.

Two men dead. They had deserved to die, they had asked for it; but that was dubious consolation to the man who had been their executioner, a man who had thought he left that sort of thing behind him years ago.

Another man – a good man in his way – was on the point of death. And a wounded younker – probably unarmed – was roaming the countryside.

And now a mysterious stranger had arrived. A gunfighter, Kate had said. Another one! *Poisonous.* A dressed-up rattlesnake.

Gabe Parker felt suddenly old again.

This was no time to feel that way. He had a premonition that the thing that had started this morning was not nearly finished yet.

He straightened his shoulders and put on a brighter face as he joined his wife and daughter in the other room.

SEVEN

BROTHER COYOTE

The sun was a ball of molten blood in a yellow sky.

Yellow? Funny colour for a sky.

Then suddenly the sun was a blazing copper gong and it filled the yellow sky, blotting it out altogether and a giant fist struck it. *Boom.* And then his brain, *his* brain: that was blood and it burst and the blood splashed and became flame and he was falling.

Then he was empty and lost.

Then he was no more.

But he came back again. *Feebly.* And there was no blood, no sun even.... But just a black shadow looming over him, blanketing everything.

Instinctively, he went for his gun. But his hand wouldn't obey his brain and he fumbled. And then he discovered there wasn't any gun, that his holster was empty. Somebody must've stolen his gun. He had had one. He had bought a new one – *somewhere* – he was sure he had.

Maybe he had dropped it. *The gun.* He tried to roll over and flame seared his shoulder and shot downwards and

43

exploded in his belly. He retched weakly in the sand. He remembered the sand then. And the sun, the terrible, blazing sun. And the yellow sky.

And the menacing shadow.

He tried to get up.

He felt the hands then.

The shadow had hands.

He must have passed out again.

Joe Gravez was a half-breed. Half-Mex, half-Apache.

He was a long way from his home-territory of New Mexico.

He didn't like this part of the West, but having once settled here, hopefully, he had never earned enough to be able to leave again.

So his Indian wife had died here and his children were growing up here, helping him with the small farm, scraping what they could, living as best they could.

Joe's plough was worn out and broken. He had been on his way to hire one from a neighbour – nobody around here ever actually *lent* Joe anything – when he found the wounded man in the sand, the palomino pony grazing on the sparse, tufted grass near him.

The man fought feebly, reached for a gun that wasn't there. A young man, little more than a sick boy, pale hair tumbling over bloodless forehead.

The wounded shoulder had been bandaged quite expertly but the wrappings had come loose with the man's fall and the wound had broken open. The wrappings were already pulpy with drying blood.

As Joe lifted the now-unconscious body on to the back of his patient old mare, Lolita, the blood began to flow badly again. Joe staunched it as best he could with a none-too-clean kerchief. He knew he must get the wounded man back to the farm before he was too far gone. The plough would have to wait.

'Home, old dog,' said Joe to Lolita.

She ambled slowly away, gentle with her burden as if she understood.

Joe had a way with animals and the palomino was quite tractable too, allowed this soft-spoken elderly man to lead him.

The younger boy, Pedro, met them first. He ran ahead to tell his fourteen-year-old sister, Maria, Joe's only daughter to prepare a bed and hot water and good soup.

Joe was strangely happy. He was glad that he and his family could do these things for this sick and lonesome stranger. He liked the look of the yellow-haired young man. The young man was going to be all right or he Jose Gero Fernando Jesus Gravez would know the reason why!

The street had drifted into late-afternoon somnolence. The shadows were long. The sun had moved to the back of Gabe Parker's place and was sinking into the rim of the wastelands. The shop was a haven of cool gloom now, restful after the blaze and violence of the morning.

Gabe worked at his bench once more.

There was no shadow this time. Just the footsteps, the clip-clop of high-heeled riding boots.

Gabe looked up. Again he could not see the visitor's face because his back was to the window. He had shut the door carefully behind him, though that door was seldom kept shut.

Another stranger. Tall this one too, taller than the other one had been. Lean. A stillness about him. A stillness and a deadliness that Gabe sensed, glad that this time he had a loaded shotgun within reach of his hand, but hoping desperately that he wouldn't have to use it again.

The man spoke and the voice was curiously toneless. Something deadly about this too.

'Hallo, Gay.'

The gunsmith felt an inward jolt. It was years since anybody had called him 'Gay'. Even his wife only called him that occasionally in their most intimate moments.

The years rolled back. He knew who the visitor was. 'Hallo, Lafe,' he said.

The tall man, taller even than Gabe himself but much thinner, moved nearer. He reached up slowly, warily almost, and took off his beautiful black sombrero. The light shone momentarily on his black hair, the blaze of silver across the top.

'So it was you,' said Gabe. 'The description the wife gave me fooled me.'

'My new trademark, you mean. A crazy Dutchman split my head with an axe. Nearly did for me....'

He paused. 'I did for him though,' he added. There was no shade of satisfaction, or anything else, in the toneless voice.

'You're some way out of your territory aren't you, Lafe?'

'I'm a rover, Gay. I've always been a rover, you know that.'

He waved his hand expansively.

'The land is mine.'

The gesture was theatrical but the voice did not vary in pitch at all.

'If you're at all as you used to be, you don't rove anyplace without a good reason,' said Gabe. 'What's your reason for coming to Benton City?'

'I came to see my old saddle-pard, Gay Penrose ... I – er – beg your pardon – Gabe Parker.'

'There must be another reason.' Gabe thought he had guessed that reason.

'Wal – all right then. Where is he?'

'Where's who?'

'You never were dumb, Gay, so don't act as if you are. Where's the yellow-haired kid you took in? Where's George Roddick?'

'Oh, so that's his name. I knew his first name was George, but I didn't get to learn his second one. I only met him this morning and we weren't formally introduced. He's gone now anyway. Pity. I should've liked to get to know him better.'

You did a lot for him in that short time, didn't you? You killed two men for him.'

'Not for him exactly. One of them trespassed in my home and threw down on me. The other attacked my wife and shot one of my best friends.'

'That drunken marshal.'

'You taken to siding with such scum, Lafe? The sort who attack women and shoot down old men?'

'Like you allus used to say, Gay: it takes all kinds. The Coyotes are riding again, Gay. Under new management, of course.'

'Of course! Wal, I'm sorry I can't help you, Lafe. Not in any way.'

'You're not going to tell me where George Roddick is?'

'I don't *know* where he is. I wished I did. Loco young fool.'

'He's around here someplace.'

'Are you callin' me a liar, Lafe?'

The other man chuckled, a sound as toneless as his voice, no mirth about it. 'What would you do if I were?'

His feet shifted a little. Then he found himself looking into the twin muzzles of Gabe's shotgun.

'I've never known you to use a shotgun before, Gabe. That was pretty fast. But are you still as fast with a handgun?'

'I don't wear one.'

'How convenient for you.'

'Get out of here, Lafe. And don't come back.'

'Is that all you have to say to your old friend, your old pupil?'

'I taught you too well. I said all I had to say to you years ago. Get away from here, Lafe. The people here distrust strangers. Particularly your kind of stranger. Particularly after what happened here this morning.'

'As to that, I'm as innocent as a new born babe.'

'Are you? Are you, Lafe?'

The weariness came back to Gabe. But he kept the shot-gun steady. He knew how fast Lafe could be. He was older, worn-looking. But he was still that much younger than Gabe that he had always been. Gabe didn't think Lafe would be fool enough to make a play now. But he had always been reck-less, unpredictable. Gabe hoped he wouldn't have to shoot him.

'I'll go, Gay. But I'll be back.'

'I wouldn't advise it.'

Lafe shrugged, turned. 'So-long,' he said.

Gabe watched him until he had disappeared through the door, closing it without emphasis behind him. Then, still cradling the shotgun, Gabe went over to the window.

Lafe had left his horse at a hitching-post a little way down the street, so that nobody at the gunsmith's would see or hear him ride in. Lafe hadn't changed much. He knew the tricks. And no doubt the years had taught him a few extra ones.

Gabe watched him ride away. What *was* he doing in this territory? What did he want with the yellow-haired younker he called George Roddick?

Gabe began to wish he hadn't been so precipitate. Handled differently, Lafe might have answered some ques-tions. Though, somehow, Gabe doubted this.

Poisonous, Kate had said. She hadn't known Lafe Bonarco before. She had known of him though. She hadn't seen him on this, his second visit. Gabe, though he didn't know whether he was doing right, decided to keep the knowledge of this second visit from her for the time being.

Maybe Lafe would decide not to come back after all.

Gabe went back to his bench, tried to immerse himself in his work. The guns, the beautiful guns....

But he was suddenly sick of guns. And he went over to the window once more and stood gazing unseeingly out.

There was nothing out there, no pictures. The pictures were all in his mind, and they were not good.

The Coyotes are riding again, Lafe had said.

EIGHT

THE EYE OF FATE

The Coyotes.

In the old days ... the name, the Coyotes, had struck terror into many hearts....

A trite phrase. Like something out of a dime novelette. Like something Easterners liked to read about a West they'd never know. But still true: Gabe hadn't realised how true until after those days, those old days, had passed; until he, at least, had finished with them.

Or thought he had finished with them!

'Twas said that sooner or later a man's past always caught up with him. That he reaped what he had sown, even if the reaping was delayed! For others took up where a man had left off. The evil weed he had planted flourished anew, and sometimes more vigorously.

He hadn't actually *planted* the weed in this case, Gabe told himself, it had just sort of 'growed of itself' as so many things had in those days. So many innocent plants had been nurtured with blood and misery until their normal growth was twisted out of all recognition. But they became giants all

50

the same, malformed and malignant.

And their roots were strong. Even after being torn out furiously, and rejected, they threw seeds, they sprouted again, they spread.

A man could turn his back on them, could shut them from his sight, could run away and try to forget them. But if he had not destroyed them completely – this was a difficult thing to do, involving yet more bloodletting – they spread and spread. They spread into the new world, the new life he was trying to build for himself.

Gabe Parker chuckled softly to himself. A harsh humourless sound.

You never could run far enough. Six and a half years ago he – with Katie and the little girl Prunella – were in Kansas. They had been there two years or more, had planned to settle there. Gabe had had a gunsmith's shop there not dissimilar to the one he had in Benton City now, larger, but not necessarily better.

Then a stranger had seen Gabe in the local saloon and had greeted him by name, his real name, Gayelord Penrose. And, when Gabe had pretended not to understand, the stranger, who had been drinking heavily, had become abusive. To shut him up, Gabe, the peaceable gunsmith, had had to hit him.

Gabe was a big strong man and the stranger's jaw had been broken. To protect his family from unpleasantness, Gabe had decided to pull up stakes.

He knew that though this first stranger, definitely no gunfighter, had not thrown down on him, that the next one – and there would inevitably be another one – might do just that.

There were many of his own generation who had reason to hate Gayelord Penrose. And there were others younger maybe – who would wonder if Penrose was really as fast as he was reputed to be, or whether he had slowed down at all in his retirement.

Learning where he was from blowhards like the now broken-jawed man they would come after him and wouldn't let up on him until they had proved they were right. Or until they were dead, victims to the gun of the man they challenged. It would take more than a broken jaw to stop that sort.

So Benton City, Montana, was the next port of call for Gabe Parker and his family. And there they had been ever since, in comparative happiness and oblivion.

Until this morning and a yellow-haired younker and....

'*Dad!*' The voice broke into his reverie.

Prunella.

She sounded impatient, as if this wasn't the first time she had called him.

'Your meal's ready!'

'I'm coming, honey.... All we ever do is eat,' he added. But she didn't laugh.

She came across the shop towards him, met him halfway. There was a little cleft of puzzlement on her smooth brow.

'Dad, who was the man who spoke to me out back? He said he was an old friend of yours.'

'Where?' said Gabe. 'When?'

Prunella looked startled. Perhaps he had sounded too abrupt. 'Why, outside. About half-an-hour ago. I was out back. He came riding by. A tall dark man on a grey pony. He asked if you were at home and I said you were probably in the shop. He said he knew the way and he rode round onto main street. Did he call on you?'

'Yes, he did. He's an old acquaintance. I wouldn't call him a friend. Nobody to bother about.'

52

'I didn't like him. I didn't like the way he looked at me.'

'Did your mother see him?'

'Not that time. But I told her about him and she said he would probably be the same man who had called at the back door earlier asking for you.'

They had reached the curtains. This area had been washed down by Gabe and there was no trace of blood on the floor now. But a man had died there this morning and nothing could wash the memory away.

Prunella became a little constrained, Gabe sensed it. But he was glad of it. It gave him a chance to change the subject.

'I hope you've got something good to eat,' he said lamely.

'Yes,' Prunella sounded absent-minded.

Gabe wondered whether Lafe had said something else to her, something unpleasant. He wanted to ask her but didn't quite know what words to use. He knew Lafe! Lafe and women!

'Woke up, have you?'

They were in the living-room and that was Kate speaking. Pretending to be furious, but not meaning any of it.

This is a fine family I've got, thought Gabe. This little family of mine.

This is a good life we have here. Nobody must be allowed to take it away from us.

It was Maria who found the diamonds.

At first she didn't know what they were. They were uncut and looked like nothing more than half-a-dozen lumps of glass.

But no man would carry mere lumps of glass so carefully hidden about his person.

They had been in a leather pocket rather clumsily sewn inside the yellow-haired gringo's pants. But low down on his hip, well-concealed; under the lower part of his holster, in fact, so that no bulge showed.

The unconscious man was in a filthy state. Covered with blood which had run from his wound and to which sand and dirt had become adhered. Maria had begun to strip him, preparatory to washing him down while her father mixed the herb poultice for the inflamed wound, when she felt the hard lumps and the tight pouch split open and the glassy lumps rolled into her plump brown hand.

Maria, at fourteen, was the eldest of Joe Gravez's four children. Since Joe's wife died Maria had been little mother to the three boys, her brothers.

To her this yellow-haired gringo who looked so pale and weak and, in his sickness, not much older than she was herself, was just another boy. Her life was elemental, natural: she felt nothing strange about stripping the unconscious man: had she felt embarrassment, the feeling would have been brand-new and she wouldn't have understood it.

'Father,' she said and laid out the diamonds in the palm of her hand.

Joe looked puzzled at first. Then he took the stones and looked at them more closely and rolled them around in his fingers and his eyes began to gleam. In his younger days in New Mexico Joe had worked for a powerful gringo merchant who did a lot of buying and selling – lawful and otherwise – of all kinds of commodities, including uncut stones.

'*Madre de Dios,*' said Joe.

He put the stones into his pocket. He didn't know what to do. He motioned to Maria to get on with her task. She was trained to obedience and she turned to her unconscious patient once more. Joe left what he had been doing and went into the sun.

He wanted to think.

But he wasn't good at thinking, he could only *feel*.

He could *see* – and *feel*.

His face was the colour of ancient nutmeg and wrinkled and immobile, he looked more Apache than Mexican. His eyes were like black buttons, very bright, very watchful.

They watched now. Watched the children playing in the dust.

Happy children, though they had so little to be happy about. But they didn't realise this.

They had never known anything else in their lives except this pin-pen of a home and the arid earth surrounding it. This, and an occasional visit to neighbouring Benton City where they were accustomed to speak softly and with lowered eyes because it was their nature and because it was what the gringos expected of them. They saw no shame in this, for they were but children. But their father saw shame, *felt* shame, knowing all the while that he had to sing small or he would not sell his meagre crop to the gringos.

He often wished he was all Indian. A fierce and proud Apache. Instead of a muddy mixture of bloods. A mixture of something that ultimately spelled *nothing*.

But even this was only 'thinking' on the most elemental plane, it was mostly *feeling*. As he felt now for his children, Maria, José, Pedro, Jesus and Fernando in their ragged clothes and bare feet.

They had never had shoes. He had always said that some-day he would get them shoes. But he had never been able to do so. And he himself only wore rope sandals, as did Maria his daughter and her patched dresses. A girl her age should have pretty things like the girls in Benton City had. Why, many of these were not nearly so plump and beautiful as Maria, which was a strange thing, for they assuredly ate much better.

Joe was not a man of quick decisions.

But he knew he had to make a quick one now.

He rose and went back into the house.

'We go,' he said, simply, to his daughter.

'Yes, papa,' she said.

She did not question his decision. She had realised from how carefully those dull lumps of glass had been hidden and from her father's reactions when she gave them to him that they must in some way be valuable. Maybe her father would be able to sell them for a lot of money.

'How about the young gringo, papa?' she asked.

Joe did not answer this question right away. Here was another decision he had to make and it was not an easy one. This wounded young gringo was a guest in his humble home. One did not rob one's guests and one did not walk away and leave them in an empty house. Particularly if they were sick as this one was.

But in this case, for more than one reason, it would not be fitting to take the gringo with them.

Joe Gravez had to weigh this gringo against his own family. An unknown gringo, a bad one probably, despite his looks. Possibly he had stolen the diamonds and had been shot while getting away with them. Fate had led him to Joe's humble home. Was Joe to spit in the eye of Fate?

The man was sleeping. His wound was dressed and he had been bathed and he did not look quite so sick as he had when Joe found him.

Joe made his decision, turned to his daughter. 'We will leave him. Burt Grogan will be by as usual. He will find him.'

'Yes, papa,' said Maria and went out to call the boys.

Burt Grogan was the ugly son of a neighbouring farmer whose land abutted the Gravez place. Richer land it was too, which gave the ill-favoured Burt and his father plenty of excuse for patronising the half-breed family. Burt had his eye on the pretty Gravez girl; though it was not conceivable that he had anything as outlandish as marriage in his mind. And, even if he had, his father, who held the purse strings, would never have countenanced such a match.

But every day while riding the line, Burt found an excuse to call in at the Gravez place and drink coffee and brag and act for all the word like the squire of an old English manor visiting his serfs. He was ugly and fat and loud and Maria cordially disliked him and sensed that her inscrutable father did so too. But neither of them revealed their dislike, for Burt's father was of some little help to them, though he was certainly not the sort to dispense charity. It was, in fact, to him that Joe had been going to hire a plough when he had found the yellow-haired stranger wounded in the sand.

Yes, Burt would surely call today. and the yellow-haired stranger would be taken care of and his neglect would not be upon Joe Gravez's conscience.

But they must hurry now before Burt arrived. Or perhaps – and this would be much more dangerous – before the arrival of the man or men who had been responsible for the yellow-haired gringo's wound.

NINE

A BROKEN LINK

Burt Grogan was surprised that he did not see the Gravez kids playing around the sagging frame house or working in the fields. Though they were more usually playing than working; no wonder this place was in such a rundown condition. Like his father always said, these people were a prime example of the shiftlessness and uselessness of mongrels, breeds, half-castes or whatever you like to call 'em. You just couldn't do anything with them. You couldn't get through to them.

Burt would go along with this last pronouncement at least. They were always polite to him but it seemed to him that there was always a wall between him and them, hardly less with the girl than with the old man. That bitch! That Maria! He'd like to get her off in the bushes. He'd strike fire from her then he'd wager or his name wasn't Burt Grogan. Big Burt who more than a dozen girls in Benton City would be glad to capture and hold.

Come to think of it, he could get plenty of girls in Benton City any time he felt like it. Then why did he bother his bones about a half-breed wench?

Burt sat his horse and called, 'Anybody to home?'

There was no reply. Nobody came out to meet him.

This was strange, for, despite that invisible wall-like reserve that Burt sensed in them, the Gravezes were always well-mannered. 'Fawning', Burt's father called it, and maybe he was right.

Burt kneed his horse forward and along the side of the house. There was no sound from inside and when he got round back there was nobody there.

Burt rode out a little way, looked out across to the horizon shimmering in the heat-haze. Nothing human moved. He got off his horse and left him there and returned to the back of the house.

There was no back door, just an irregular square hole hacked in the adobe wall and covered with a gunny sack. It was low down, half-window half-door. Burt lifted a corner of the sack to one side and peered in. After the glare of the sun, the gloom was so deep that he couldn't see a thing. Nothing moved. He let the dust-stinking improvised curtain fall. He could easily have climbed through the aperture, but he had his pride.

He glanced back at his horse, grazing contentedly on the sparse grass out there. Burt decided to leave the beast were he was.

Trying to temper his usual heavy-footedness, Burt went round to the front of the cabin again. Maybe old man Gravez had gone suddenly loco and, wanting to protect his daughter's honour was waiting behind the door with a shotgun.

Burt's heavy, ugly face split in a broken-toothed grin. He almost guffawed aloud.

Even so, his hand was on the butt of his gun as he approached the door.

The silence was oppressive. Flies buzzed in the heavy late-afternoon sunshine. The tiny sounds were all a part of the stillness.

Burt's throat was dry, his voice hoarse as he called, 'Ain't anybody about?'

He sounded almost plaintive.

There was no reply. No sound from the cabin, from behind the closed door.

It wasn't usually closed like this, Burt reflected., The whole place had a blind, brooding shut-in look. Was somebody playing games? With a sudden gust of fury, he grabbed the latch, lifted it, flung the door open with a crash.

Dust drifted from sagging rafters. But nothing else happened.

Burt stepped inside. The small place was like the inside of a furnace. Burt blinked in the sun-dappled gloom.

He saw the man on the bunk and he drew his gun.

Then he stood foolishly, the weapon sagging in his fist. He realised that the reclining man was still; harmless. Maybe he was dead.

What devil's business had these half-breeds been at?

Burt looked around the main room, such as it was. Then he crossed it and peered into the small two-room lean-to. The only sleeping accommodation. A pair of foetid cupboards.

The birds had flown all right. There were only the flies and a small, sleepy green lizard who blinked harmlessly from a corner.

Burt returned to the man in the bunk.

He was still alive. He was wounded, sleeping. Sleeping very deeply. Burt did not recognise the pallid young face beneath the wild yellow hair. A saddle tramp. In a bad way too, though evidently somebody had been doctoring him recently, bandaging him.

Surely the Gravezes hadn't wounded him first and

doctored him afterwards.

Though who could tell about them and their strange half-Indian ways!

Shaking his head lowly from side to side, Burt began a cursory search of the sleeping man.

He noted the empty holster.

And the stranger was not only minus a gun, he was minus everything else except the clothes he lay in, and they were no great shakes and he wore only tattered moccasins on his feet instead of the usual scuffed riding boots.

Burt made a cursory search of the cabin too, making swipes at things like a petulant bear.

There was a pan full of soup on the hearth. A small fire glowed. The soup was still warm, didn't look as if any had been used.

Had the soup been intended for the wounded man? If so, what had made the Gravez brood light out so suddenly without feeding it to him?

Burt kicked at the stove and punished his big toe a bit; he lurched over to the window, cursing. Through the dirty misshapen patches of glass he saw the riders approaching, wavy and indistinct like a sand mirage.

But they were no mirage.

Burt stopped his mouthing. Trying to keep himself hidden as much as possible he moved closer to the window. He almost pressed his nose against the glass.

There were four riders. They were a hard-looking bunch and Burt didn't think he had ever seen any of them before.

He watched them dismount and approach the cabin. He was glad he had left his horse at the back of the place where these people couldn't spot him. They looked as if they were up to no good. They fanned out. They walked with their hands close to their guns, ready for action.

Burt moved back into one of the cubby-holes. The one, slightly the larger, which had the aperture in its back wall with the gunny sack hung across it.

He drew his gun and stood in the gloom and waited.

He heard the door open, the thudding of boots on the hard-packed dirt floor. Then a voice said:

'By all that's holy, here he is.'

Another voice said, 'He ain't dead, is he?'

'No, he ain't dead.'

Then all four voices seemed to be speaking at once. Until an authoritative one rose above the others.

'Hold it!'

There was silence then, except for a fair amount of boot-scraping.

Then the louder voice spoke again. Authoritative, yet strangely toneless, strangely chilling.

'He ain't got the stones on him. Look – he must've had 'em sewn inside his pants. The pocket's empty now.... Crane, take a look out back of this hole.'

Burt Grogan didn't stop to hear any more. He almost dived through the aperture, leaving the gunny-sack flapping wildly in its own dust. He ran clumsily. He was almost at his horse when he heard the yell; then there was the sound of a shot. The slug passed uncomfortably near, he heard the whine of it.

He mounted into the saddle. He looked back. The man had climbed through the hole. He was the tallest of the four. A regular beanpole. Burt took a shot at him and missed. He put spurs to his horse, knowing the bunch would take time to get to their own mounts. If they chased him into his own territory, his own boys would soon take care of 'em.

But he didn't intend to let any of the four get into shoot-

62

ing range again if he could help it. He rowelled his mount savagely.

The galloping horse stepped into a gopher hole and fell heavily. Burt was pitched over the beast's neck, travelled headfirst, hit the sun-baked earth with crushing force. His neck was broken immediately and completely and finally.

His horse, miraculously unhurt, galloped madly away..

Lace Branch and his boys searched the corpse but they did not find the precious stones they sought.

'I don't figure him to be the sort who'd live in a sod hut like that one back there. Maybe he was just visiting and he found the place empty the same as we did. Except for young George that is.'

It was the beanpole, Crane speaking; 'Crane' only being a mighty appropriate nickname for him.

'Yeh,' said Lace. 'I figure the folks who own that hut picked up George and doctored him. An' they found the stones an' lit out with them. But which way, that's the rub? We better try an' read some sigh. Gabby!'

Gabby was the half-breed member of the bunch. He seldom spoke, hence his nickname, appropriate like Crane's, though in a backhanded way.

'That way,' he growled, nodding his head.

His lean face was like grooved mahogany. He'd been looking for sign all along it seemed. Maybe he'd had it all figured out from the time they found the cabin and the unconscious George Roddick. Someday I'm going to kill that goddamned Indian, thought Lace, but without undue emotion.

'All right, let's go.'

'How about George?' said the fourth man, a hairy ape called Summer. Just Summer, nobody knowing whether this was his first or his last name.

Summer wasn't too bright and he liked hurting people.

He had been looking forward to working on young George, making him talk.

'We've no time to waste. We'll leave him,' said Lace. 'He ain't going anyplace.'

'If he gets over that wound the crazy fish'll come right after us,' said Crane.

'I'll look forward to that then,' said Lace.

They left the body of Burt Grogan behind and moved in the direction Gabby had indicated.

The half-breed – his grandfather had been a Piute – got off his horse from time to time and sniffed around like a prairie-dog on the scent of something good.

The three other men watched him impatiently but did not interfere. He was the best tracker any of them had ever known. He was invaluable in a situation like this. There was too much at stake now for them to gripe about Gab's manners.

Their prize had been snatched from under their noses by a yellow-haired scut hardly out of kneebritches. Two men had died since; and still the prize eluded them. Killers all, they were in a rabid mood now; even Gabby, despite his surly lack of haste. They meant to get what they were after this time, if they had to kill a whole town to do it.

TEN

THE VICTIM

The gringo merchant for whom Joe Gravez worked in New Mexico in the old days had been a retired sea-captain. He died at a comparatively early age. For all the wealth he accrued in the later years, and the fine food and houses and clothes and comfort it bought, shore life never really suited him.

While pacing one of his own palatial wharves he trod on a rusty nail which penetrated his boot and half-an-inch into his flesh.

The ex-captain died suddenly and miserably from blood poisoning.

There was no bequest for his faithful half-caste servant Joe Gravez – Jose as he was then.

So Joe helped himself to the one thing that 'the Cap'n' (his own name for his boss) had always promised him. The long, powerful shining brass telescope.

The telescope was still his. It was one of the few things he took with him when, all these years later, he and his family left their adobe cabin in Montana.

It was a flight. But a slowish one. They only had two horses between five people. An old man; a girl, and three children: three boys. Not a heavy girl, though comely. Surprisingly comely considering that she had never been particularly well-fed.

But the three boys were skinny. Nobody could truthfully say they were not skinny.

But two horses between five people – even maybe between two and three half-people – there indeed was a problem. The nature of these two horses was so different also, that was another thing.

Lolita now: she was getting long in the tooth; she was still strong; but she had never been fast. She was the phlegmatic, plodding, patient kind. But the palomino – the yellow-haired young stranger's palomino – he was a different mess of fish altogether. He was fast and skittish and temperamental.

Where as on their first encounter he had been quite tractable, now – and this perhaps because he had been fed since – it took all Joe's considerable skill with horseflesh to curb his wild mischief. And, still, every now and then he bucked with vicious glee or skirled off at a tangent as if startled by invisible sidewinders.

He objected to having two riders at once, even if they were only children. He threw two of the boys quite heavily and the incensed Joe swiped at him with the brass telescope but, luckily, missed.

It was years since Joe had held the telescope, let alone wielded it in such a way. In any case, he had had no reason to use it – in any way – over the last long years in that flat terrain which had been his home: a sameness for unknowable miles, a flatness even as far as the Grogan spread where the earth was richer, the pasture greener.

But there was reason to use the telescope now.

A bid. Maybe a desperate one; maybe not. Who could tell? A *flight*. A hill hiding from their sight the land which they had already traversed. A halt. And Joe climbing the hill with the telescope.

The lens were dusty. He polished them with his kerchief. Then he raised the cool brass rim to his eye. It kissed the lids. It brought back old memories. At first he had difficulty in getting things into focus. Then, even when he did, all he could see was the shimmering plain, the sky going purple on the horizon. At first.

Then he saw the dust-cloud. At first it looked just a smoky puff-ball. Because of the distance it seemed motionless. But Joe kept his gaze riveted on it. So hard that the brass rim of the telescope began to hurt his eye, was no longer cold, began to stick with the sweat.

Madre de Dios. Yes, there was a bunch of riders all right. Half-a-dozen. Not more, maybe less. But coming this way. And faster than Joe and his children could ever hope to travel, for inevitably the pace was set by the slower mount, Lolita, and both horses bore double burdens.

Joe stood a few seconds. Were those riders after him? Again – who could tell? He was a fatalist. If they *were* after him, so be it; they were. But one should be prepared.

He scrambled down the hill.

He told his children – all four of them – what they must do. The girl, Maria took the package of stones. But still she argued. This was not like Maria. There was fear in her beautiful dark eyes. Fear for her father. Until in desperation, and near-panic, he raised his hand and struck her.

Then she led the boys away, two of them mounted on the palomino, the eldest walking beside her.

Turning once to look back, her gaze steadfast for a small pause of time.

They did not wave. Then going on, the palomino tractable for a while.

And Joe moving too. Mounting Lolita. With the telescope, the bundles. Riding on at Lolita's pace. No slower, no faster. Deviating here and there. Finding the dustier patches, creating his own little dust-cloud, the first thing the riders would see when they came round the edge of the hill.

And Joe hoped that by that time Maria and the boys, on a different trail, using all the cover they could find, would be out of sight.

God speed them then; God go with them.

Once the riders turned the base of the hill and saw their quarry they quickly caught up with him. They surrounded him and Lafe knocked him from his horse. They dismounted and clustered over him, like vultures. They searched him thoroughly, tearing his meagre clothing.

Again they did not find what they wanted. They vented their fury on him. But their methods were not systematic enough for Lafe and he called them off. Then he sent the ape-like Summer in alone.

Summer paused momentarily, calculating. Then Lafe made an impatient gesture and Summer bent over the small, elderly, feeble-struggling man. Summer straddled his victim.

George Roddick had been vaguely aware of hands plucking at him. At different periods of time. The world seemed full of hands. Clutching, demanding, pulling. But he was too sick to care, too tired, too much out of this world.

But, ultimately, his spirit would not allow him to give up completely and he began to come to himself, to feel himself, to be himself again.

Not completely himself, may be, but at least a recognisable image, a fighting spirit again, if only a comparatively feeble one.

68

He remembered his wounded shoulder and it was stiff. But it did not burn now. There was warmth all around him but it did not seem to be coming from the sun for there was no glare. In the back of his mind he had the idea that he had done some travelling, though not completely under his own steam. He had left the sun anyway – he could've died beneath the sun – and now he was in some enclosed space.

And now he became like an animal, lying doggo, keeping his eyes closed, listening.

The hands had gone away, the plucking fingers. How many pairs of hands? He could feel nothing now. Nothing but the dull stiff ache of his shoulder. He could hear nothing.

He could smell though, enclosed heat, cooking odours. And sour earth and the tang of people living together and sleeping and breathing and sweating. The silence was thick, redolent, so that he felt he could cut it. But it was silence for all that: it was unbroken by human sounds.

He opened his eyes slowly.

The impact of everything upon him was immediate. The smells, the enclosed heat, the light of the window. He rolled; he retched weakly over the edge of the bunk. He lay supine and slowly began to feel better. The ache of his shoulder became a pain, a grinding agony. But the pain was sweet, it was alive and pulsating. He struggled upwards, swung his feet from the bunk. The process was slow, he did not force it. He let his feet dangle gently – oh, so gently – until they touched the floor. Then he rested awhile, his hands pressed against the bunk, until things were easier again.

Then before he attempted anything else, he lifted his right hand a little and felt among his clothing.

The secret pocket was open. The stones were gone.

He began to laugh softly. The tears trickled slowly down his cheeks. Trying to stop himself shaking, he felt as if he were breaking into pieces.

But finally the spasm passed and, after a couple of false tries, to his great amazement he was able to stand up.

His world had crumbled a little. He was a poor lopsided coot upon the surface of it. But his world had not completely blown up, he was still part of it, still alive, still fighting. He was a poor robber, a robber robbed, but he was not finished yet.

He wandered over to the hearth. There was stew in a pan and he heated it up, sitting on a convenient broken-backed chair.

Finding a spoon among other utensils on a dusty shelf, he ate wolfishly.

He discovered that his wound had been re-bandaged and this puzzled him a little. If the owner of the hut had stolen the loot – and it certainly looked that way – why hadn't he put paid to George completely too? Maybe he had figured that George was finished anyway, and left him here to die. He wouldn't be the first one to be fooled by the yellow-haired young man's look of apparent fragility. And then there had been the wound!

George felt light-headed. He figured he had probably had a fever and had got over it. Maybe it *had* been touch and go for a while and the hombre who took the stones *had* made a good guess. But, for all that, he had guessed wrong. George was still very much alive, if not exactly kicking.

George found his way to the door and looked outside. There was no horse. Nothing but the flat plains spreading out to the blue haze of approaching dusk. He turned. By easy stages he explored the small abode. Despite his snail-like pace, this didn't take long. He had a short rest, then found his way out and round back. He even got as far as the privy, where he was sick again, cursing, fetching up the stew he had so recently taken.

70

He sat out there for a while as the blue dusk closed around him and the temperature lowered. Nothing and nobody bothered him for a while. Then he began to shiver and he got up and made his slow way back to the 'dobe hut.

He blew on the fire and added some sticks, found coffee in a can, water in a pitcher. He made himself a brew and found some hard biscuits and filled the gap in his belly again, sipping at the scalding-hot black coffee.

He began to feel better. He went and lay on the bunk, the better to think things out. Though this didn't help much.

He had to face things. No horse, no gun, no money. And a hole in his shoulder which right now was giving him hell. Good clean hell though, fortunately. What you might call healthy hell. Not the kind of hell that would kill him, he thought, though maybe it had been touch and go for a while.

Come to think of it, he would have been a goner long since if the gunsmith back in town hadn't backed him. Some man that gunsmith. And that daughter of his. Taking all that trouble over a saddle-tramp like him – a thief, just a thief.

He began to see things with a new clarity. He wondered how far it was to the town. What was it called? Benton City?

Some city!

But where else could he go without a horse? He couldn't stay here, that was too dangerous. He'd have to walk. Though he didn't feel like walking, he was lucky he wore moccasins instead of high-heeled riding boots which would be crippling him after the first mile.

He wasn't quite sure he knew in which direction Benton City lay. But having lived his life in the open spaces of the West, he was willing to trust to his inherent sense of direction to steer him right. He could not just lie here, that was for sure.

Like this he was a sitting duck.

A *reclining* duck.

He began to giggle, shake, felt himself beginning to get light-headed again. He fought this, let himself slide from the bunk, his feet hitting the hard-packed dirt floor with a force that shook him from head to foot.

Pain stopped his giggling. He wanted to lie down again, but willed himself not to do so. He went over to the hearth, poured himself more coffee and drank it quickly. It was luke-warm now, black and treacly, too strong. It had a kick like a vicious mule and did him plenty of good.

He foraged again, found more biscuits, a few strips of dried beef. These smelt a bit peculiar but he held on to them. He found a small paper sack with a few spoonfuls of flour. He put the rest of his meagre haul in with this and then as an after-thought added the can of coffee. Then the sack was full.

He had no water-canteen, couldn't find one. By this time he was groping around in the dark. Finally, however, he found a dusty old bottle and swilled it out and filled it with water from the pitcher. Then he was all set and, before he could change his mind, he set out.

ELEVEN

THE HUNTERS

'Let him be, you crazy skunk,' said Lafe. 'Can't you see he's dead? He hit his head on that boulder.'

At Lafe's words the brutish Summer backed away like a dog reprimanded by his master. He stood in sullen silence, his big hands hanging impotently.

The half-breed, Gabby bent over the huddled form of Joe Gravez.

'He's dead all right.' The light was fading. There was a coldness, a stillness. The four standing men, the crumpled one at their feet, were like lost people in a empty world suspended in time.

Lafe Bonarco had taken off his hat. The blaze of silver gleamed dully in the black mane of his hair.

He said: 'Take him in among those rocks. Cover him up, hide him.... Summer, stir yourself. You haven't finished yet.'

The ape-like man grunted, shambled forward. He and Gabby carried the body among the rocks. Crane and Lafe waited impatiently. Then when the two returned, Lafe said:

'It'll soon be dark. There isn't anything we can do right

now. That old jasper has really fixed us.'

There was no humour in his voice, no tone at all.

'Maybe he just didn't know where the stones are,' said Crane.

Next to Lafe he was the intelligent one of the bunch. Even before the other two died on the dusty street of Benton City, Crane had been Lafe's right-hand man. The two men killed by Gabe Parker had been just gunhawks; but now the strength of the band was less and Crane wondered whether Lafe meant to get reinforcements, whether they'd need any.

They were in an alien territory now. But Crane, no more than Lafe, didn't mean to leave it till they had the stones. They'd gone through a lot for that loot, by God they had; everything had gone haywire.

Lafe made no rejoinder to Crane's remark, but said:

'Better bring that goddamned old nag along. We'll move on a bit until it's dark an' then we'll camp. We'll come back here in the morning and try and pick up some sign. We know there were others with that ol' buzzard – probably they've got the stones, though why he gave them to 'em in the first place I can't figure.'

Crane had a theory about this too, but he kept his mouth shut this time. Lafe's voice was as toneless as ever, it never varied. But Crane had spent many years in close proximity to the man with the silver blaze and he could sense when Lafe was at boiling point. And that was the time he was most dangerous. He was the fastest and most terrible man with a gun that Crane had ever known, and the lean man had ridden with some hard ones in his time and was no mean fighter himself.

They moved on, Gabby leading the old mare, Lolita.

Go to Gabe Parker, papa had said. Mr Parker was a good man.

He is an honest man too, papa had said: give him the stones, he will know what to do.

Maria was very tired when she knocked on the back door of the gunsmith's, for she had walked while the boys took it in turns to ride the palomino. She had run too, until she could run no more. But she had driven herself on, step by step.

It was dark now and the heat of the day had suddenly gone and there was a cool wind.

It was black out there; the stars were pinpricks high in the sky so they gave little light. There was no moon. And out there her father remained and Maria couldn't bear to think what might have happened to him.

So she started to jabber tearfully as soon as Mr Parker opened the door and she did not notice the big man had a shotgun in the crook of his arm.

Gabe peered at her. 'It's Maria, the Gravez girl,' he called and his wife appeared at his shoulder, her white hair shining in the beams of the lamp inside.

'Come in. Is that the boys there with you? Come in all of you.'

Gabe stood aside and Kate put her arm round the girl's shoulders. The three boys followed, José, Jesus and the baby, Fernando. All talking at once, tearfully; in their anxiety jabbering in a mixture of Spanish and American.

'Take it slow,' said Gabe. 'Take it slow.'

Kate sat Maria down. Prunella brought her a glass of water. Gabe stood, half-puzzled now, just inside the half-open door. He had spotted the horse outside, the palomino. And this one had a blanket thrown over its back instead of a saddle. Just the way the crippled hostler, Barnaby Jimson, had described the palomino rode by the yellow-haired stranger called George.

Maria sipped her water. She got a hold of herself and snapped at the boys in Spanish until they became silent. Then she told her story.

'I better go get some men together,' said Gabe.

He handed his shotgun to Kate. 'We'll be all right,' she said, answering his unspoken question. 'You go look for Joe Gravez.'

'I'll get Big Lon, Barnaby, the mayor, the doc,' Gabe was already on his way out. Passing through the shop he got his coat and the hair-trigger pistol that by rights belonged to George Roddick, the owner of the palomino.

Gabe's own horse was in the lean-to. Gabe slung a saddle on the beast's back, working fast, an excitement working in him that he tried hard to kill. This was like the old days. But he was cool really; he told himself that he never really got het-up. Experience had told him long since that a man had to keep cool in a crisis. He would have been buzzard bait years ago if he hadn't always kept his head.

Ten minutes later he led his improvised posse from Benton City. The men he had already enumerated. Big Lon Stafler, blacksmith; Barnaby Jimson, livery-stableman; Ed Cranthorpe, unofficial mayor; and tall Doc Crane who strode a horse like a prince and was afraid of no man. Doc might be needed, and not only for fighting. As for the other three: Ed was a peppery little cuss and he could use a gun; Big Lon was no gunman but a giant in a brawl; the crippled Barnaby could use a gun if need be and, Gabe suspected, use it better than any of the others except Gabe himself.

They rode into the night. Rode in the direction of the outcrop of rock Maria had described to Gabe, the small land-mark that all of them knew well.

Gabe rode in the forefront. The years rolled back for him. The old freedom was there, the old urge. He had led men like this before. Hunters galloping through the night. The motion of a speeding horse, the wind in his face, good fighting men at his back. He had led better men than this bunch, he had led some real wolves. But these were good men in other ways and they would not be found wanting; he tried to forget the other sort.

Barnaby Jimson, as part compensation for his twisted body, had eyes and ears like a cat. It was he who called, 'Hold it! There's something over there.'

They reined in.

'Where?' said Gabe.

'It was a man,' said Barnaby. 'I'm sure it was. But he didn't have a horse.'

'I can't see anything,' said Ed Cranthorpe pompously. 'Who'd be out here at this time o' night without a horse?'

'He's behind that clump o' brush over there,' said Barnaby. 'There's no other place he could hide.'

'Let's take a look then.' Gabe kneed his horse forward.

'We're wasting time,' said Ed Cranthorpe. But, with the others, he followed.

Realising that further concealment was impossible the man showed himself.

'I'm seeing things,' said Gabe and there was but little humour in his voice.

The yellow-haired younker, George Roddick stood swaying before him, a scarecrow in the night.

Peering up at the horsemen owlishly.

'Howdy, folks,' said George Roddick, and he pitched forward on his face.

They all dismounted. Doc Craven was first at his patient. He made a quick examination and cursed softly.

'This one must be loco roaming about in the middle of the night with a wound like that.'

Barnaby Jimson and Gabe Parker exchanged puzzled glances. Both of then had seen more of George Roddick than the others had.

Gabe was even more puzzled than the little hostler. Questions teemed through his head. He knew that Maria back at his home probably had the answers to most of them. She had not told him much, only that her father was in terrible danger. That had been enough for Gabe, he hadn't waited for any more.

'You folks go on,' said Doc Craven. 'I'll take him back to town. He needs fixing up as soon as possible. I hate to leave, but …'

'You go, Doc,' said Gabe Parker sharply. 'Your job's with the sick, we all know that.'

The others chorused assent. Big Lon Stafler lifted George Roddick as if he was a baby and laid him across the saddle of the doc's horse. George mumbled a little but did not unduly complain. Doc mounted behind him, waved a parting hand.

The other four men set their mounts at the gallop again. They did not look back at the doc and his slowly moving horse, his burden. Doc had his task, they had yet to find theirs.

They reached their destination and reined in. There was silence but for the soughing of the wind. They set their horses back into cover. Then they hid themselves and began to look among the rocks.

Again it was Barnaby who heard the sounds. They led their horses back into cover. Then they hid themselves in the rocks and drew their guns and waited.

Kate Parker held the stones in the hollowed palm of her hand. They gleamed dully beneath the lamplight.

78

'They do not look much,' said Maria. 'But I think they are precious.'

'They are,' said Kate. 'I've seen one like them before. They're uncut diamonds. They must be worth a fortune.'

'Are you sure, mother?' asked Prunella.

'Yes, I'm sure.' Kate nearly added that she had known men who would kill for but one stone like these, but because of Maria she did not do so.

Maria had told her full story by now. Kate remembered the wounded young man with the yellow hair. He had left a note on the kitchen table. Kate still had the scrap of paper in the pocket of her apron. He had not wanted to bring trouble to the Parker family. But he had brought trouble to the Gravez family it seemed, though, according to Maria, it had not been wholly his fault.

Kate suspected that the riders who had been following Joe Gravez and his family had been those whom the yellow-haired young man had feared or, at least, had been striving to avoid.

There must have been a gang of them – Kate had an idea that the stranger with the silver blaze in his hair was probably their leader. Her husband, Gabe, had killed two of them, but there were surely others. And now Kate knew what they were after. And she feared for her husband and for the others. And for poor Joe Gravez who, though maybe a covetous old man, did not deserve the terrible things that could, or perhaps already had, happened to him.

The three boys were asleep, bedded down in blankets behind the counter in the shop, their own little hidey-hole. They were children and this was new and they had been very tired.

But the girl Maria was a child no longer, she was solemn and adult for her age. Wide-eyed and anxious she sat and waited. She seemed to have forgotten about the stones, which

Kate placed now on the edge of the kitchen table. Lumps of glassy matter, such little things to cause such bloodshed and death and misery. How had the young George got them, Kate wondered; was he just a yellow wolf after all, a yellow-haired lobo wolf?

And the girl sat staring into space.

Kate felt like grabbing the dully-shining stones and marching to the door and flinging the handful out piecemeal into the night, scattering them. There was something evil about them, lying there, dully winking beneath the light. They were a symbol of everything evil that had happened this day, so much evil in such a short time.

To Kate it was as if the old days were back with a greater virulence. And they had been so happy, the three of them, her and Prunella and Gabe, here in Benton City.

In a way, they had fought for their position here. After Jules Benton died and the scum left the territory, they had still been 'foreigners', mistrusted by the older settlers. But they were respected now and other 'foreigners' had come since and had been, if grudgingly at first, accepted by one and all. And now the Parker family had become part of the old guard and Gabe himself, his past buried, had become one of the leaders of the community along with Lon Staflen, Ed Cranthorpe and Doc Craven.

But the past is never really buried, thought Kate; she had realised this as she watched her husband leave tonight, swiftly and efficiently, a hunter, a professional, a gunfighter.

She took the stones up in her hand but she did not toss them away. She merely said quietly, 'I'll put these in a safe place.'

She wished she could put herself and her family and this poor girl and her brothers all in a safe place where they could stay forever.

But things had started again, as in her heart of hearts she had known they would someday. The men were out riding again. And all she could do, as she had done so many times before through the years, was hope that her man would come home safe.

TWELVE

THE THIEF

'Hold it right there,' called Gabe Parker. 'Every man's covered.'

There were five riders, a big man on a big horse at their head. He reined in, his hand raised. His followers grouped behind him. They were too much out in the open, too close together: for them to have tried anything would have been sheer suicide and evidently their leader realised this.

But would one of his more foolhardy men try something from the back there?

Things hung in the balance for a fraction of time. The wind soughed. Bridles jingled as horses stirred restlessly. Then Barnaby Jimson spoke up, as Barnaby, small and twisted but volatile, so often did.

'They're no outlaws, Gabe. That's old Sam Grogan an' some of his boys.'

'So it is,' said Gabe softly. Then he raised his voice again.

'Sam. You, Sam!'

'Who is that?' bellowed the big man on the big horse. 'Goddamn it, who are you? What's the meaning o' this?'

'This is Gabe Parker, Sam. You hear me?'

'I hear you, Gabe. What in tarnation do you think you're playing at?'

'We made a mistake, Sam. We mistook you an' your boys for somebody else. Hold your hosses – we're coming out.'

The four men rose to their feet and advanced from the rocks. Then Barnaby Jimson spotted the long ominous bundle slung over the front of one of the horses and he said:

'What's that?'

'It's my son, Burt,' said old Sam, his deep voice hoarse with emotion. 'We found him back a-ways. Looks like his horse threw him. Neck's broken. The horse came home alone and we came out lookin'.'

There was nothing more to say and the big rancher reverted to his earlier queries. 'What's going on out here? Who are those mysterious riders you're talking about, Gabe?'

'Some boys who raised hell in Benton City,' said Gabe.

'I heard there's been a killing back there today,' said one of the men. 'I heard....'

Gabe interrupted him. 'We think these hardcases got hold of old Joe Gravez. They....'

It was old Sam's turn to interrupt. 'I ain't interested in what happened to that goddamned breed! If my son hadn't been messing around his hovel like a cur after that Gravez bitch he might be alive now.' His voice rose to a sort of bellow. 'Come on, boys, we gotta get Burt back home where he belongs.'

'We're sorry about your son, Sam,' said Gabe Parker. 'Mighty sorry.'

The other three spoke their condolences too in their several ways, though young Burt had not been a very likeable sort of cuss. But they respected old Sam, the roaring father; they felt for him as they watched him ride away, with his only child bumping on a saddle like a sack of meat, though less useful than a sack of meat now. Old Sam had set great store by that boy. Some folk had said Burt would come to a bad end. But it was sort of ironical that he, a good horseman if nothing else, should finish in such a silly way.

'I thought I'd found something back there,' said Ed Cranthorpe soberly. 'Then that bunch rode up.'

He clambered over the rocks, puffing a bit, plump but light on his feet. The others followed him.

Ed scurried around a bit, not looking at all like the mayor of a so-called 'city'. But finally he said, 'Here,' and he bent his small and corpulent body.

The others joined him. With their bare hands they moved rocks and soil and then uncovered the grave of Joe Gravez. They straightened up then and looked at each other in the darkness and said nothing. Then little Barnaby Jimson bent over again.

'I don't think he's been shot. Looks to me as if he was battered to death – though that stuff they put on top of him didn't help him none. One thing, I figure he was already dead when they did that though.'

'Yeh, that's some consolation, ain't it?' said Lon Staflen savagely.

He had worked like a giant, shifting most of the heavy stuff. He had liked the quiet little half-breed, and if he could get his hands on the people who had done this he would do some real battering himself.

'Let's get moving,' he said.

'Yes,' said Gabe Parker. 'Cover Joe again, gently. He'll be safe here till we get back.'

If we get back, he might have said. He knew the men who had done this, knew their leader anyway and he was not the sort to be easily caught.

Had Gabe but known it then, Lafe Bonarco and his boys were already in hiding.

They heard old Sam Grogan and his riders moving in the distance and they changed their direction and doubled back and went to earth in a small draw. They finally bedded down with no hot drink, no fire. Lafe was too old and wily a coyote to be caught through his own lack of foresight and caution.

So Gabe Parker and his posse ranged the plains till early light and saw no signs of their quarry.

'They're probably in another state by now,' said Lon Staflen disappointedly.

'I guess you're right,' said Gabe.

Had they got what they were after, Gabe asked himself. Would they ever return?

He did not learn the answer to these two questions until he reached home. Then, after listening to Kate {Maria was asleep at last}, he knew Lafe and his boys would indeed be back and now he knew why. He rolled the diamonds around in his fingers and cursed.

He would not take breakfast yet, would not take a nap. He hurried down to Doc Craven's place to see the lean medico and his new patient, leaving Kate the unenviable task of telling the Gravez kids about their father, whose battered body now lay in Grif Kallis's undertaking parlour.

'He looks sort of puny,' said the doc. 'But I swear he must be made of some kind of leather, pickled in alcohol I wouldn't wonder, seeing as he's drunk half a bottle of my whisky already.'

'He can talk, then?'

'Yes, he can talk.'

'Lead the way,' said Gabe grimly.

Intrigued somewhat, Doc Craven led his friend into the

85

back room where George Roddick was sitting propped up against a mound of pillows in the narrow bed, his shoulder bulky, his arm in a white sling.

He grinned from the pale face beneath a mess of yellow hair. 'Howdy, Mr Parker,' he said. 'Again I'm mighty obliged to you – and to your friends an' the doc here. You always seem to show up when you're needed. If it hadn't been for you, Mr Parker, I'd've been a real gone goose by now.'

'Soft soap'll get you no place right now,' Gabe told him, then, as George's face mirrored genuine or pretended puzzlement, 'You've got a whole lot of explaining to do, young fellah. Talk!'

'I think I get your drift, sort of, Mr Parker. But I don't rightly know where to start.'

'The stones are at my place,' said Gabe. 'Tell me first how you got them. Then tell me how come a certain lobo wolf called Lafe Bonarco has his pack after you. Or did Lafe come *before* the stones maybe?'

'You know Lafe, Mr Parker?'

'I knew Lafe when you were a squawling pup. He's a killer pure and simple and if he's after you you're lucky you ain't dead already.'

'I'm lucky all right,' said George. He sighed. 'Wal, I guess I better start from the beginning and tell you all about it.'

Gabe sat on the foot of the bed. The Doc, silent, a good listener, took a chair against the wall.

'I met Lafe Bonarco in Yuma State Penitentiary,' said George.

He paused, but neither of the men said anything, just sat intent, ready to keep listening. He went on:

'He was doing five for robbery. He'd got off lightly I guess, a hellion like him. I was in for stabbing a man. It happened in a little town on the Pecos. A mud hole, a stinkin' little hell-

86

hole. I disremember the name of it now, that isn't important anyway. We had taken off our guns, me an' this other hombre an' it was supposed to be a fist-fight. But he pulled a knife and I took it off him and stuck him with it. He was like to die. I heard later he lost the use of his right arm. Anyway, I was a stranger in that town an' he was well-known – the way the cards were stacked I guess I was lucky I only got two years.

'I shared a cell with Lafe Bonarco and a half-loco ape called Summer. He was Lafe's bully boy, did everything Lafe told him. Lafe was a big man in the pen, a leader, he even had plenty of the guards dancing to his tune. I admired him I guess – an' on top o' that I was sore about the raw deal that had been handed to me.

'The three of us came out about the same time. I joined up with 'em. Lafe recruited a few more boys. A lanky cuss called Crane. Crane's the only one of 'em I can say anything good about now. He's a killer but he's a straight-shooter. Sort of decayed Southern gem'mun. Know what I mean, Mr Parker?'

'I know what you mean, son.'

Gabe had met plenty like Crane. The West was full of them after the civil war. Gabe had been one of them himself. Most of them were living fragments of a defeated and scattered army. They had no job, no home, so they took what they could get – literally.

They used the tools of the trade they had learned through the war years and they used those tools well, were dubious soldiers of fortune. They sold their guns to the highest bidder. They were robbers and killers who lived by a code: never let down a friend, always give the other feller an even break.

The West was their market place and their battleground. Their numbers were legion, the fastest and cleverest among

them became a living legend. Such had been Gayelord
Penrose, thought Gabe {Gay}, bitterly. Such was this man
Crane and the other man, Lafe Bonarco: and many of them,
like Lafe, had gone rotten, had turned into rampaging wolves
with bloodstained fangs.

George was talking again.

'There'sa half-breed called Gabby – 'cos he isn't. An'
there's – there *was*, I should say, Grimmond an' Pales.
They're the two who tried to bushwhack me, Mr Parker, the
two you cut down....'

'Yes,' said Gabe. 'And so there's four left in the gang now.'

'That's right – unless Lafe recruits more to make up for
Grimmond and Pales. Though that ain't gonna be so easy in
this territory where he ain't known.'

George paused. Then he went on again:

'We knocked over a couple of banks, did a few hold-ups.
Lafe planned the jobs well. We got away with all of 'em. I say
we, though I didn't take such a hell of a part in any of 'em if
truth's told. I was the youngest by far; the kid; Lafe's pupil,
resented by the others – except by Crane, I guess. An' Lafe
sometimes tried to treat me like he treated that half-wit,
Summer, like some kind of dog. An' I wouldn't stand for this
an' there was a friction about that sometimes.. An' I think
Summer was jealous of me. Although we had shared the same
cell for years back in the pen, he acted like he hated my guts.

'Still, I got the jobs that I guess Summer would've handled
if I hadn't been there. I resented them sometimes, though I
figured I could do 'em better than Summer ever would. I
watched the places, listened, worked out timetables, held the
horses, boiled the coffee, cooked the grub. I never took a
proper part in any job....'

'You're lucky,' said Gabe softly. 'You ain't got the blood of
innocent folks on your conscience.'

'Maybe you're right,' said George. 'But I was a member of the gang after all. I....'

'Let's not argue about ethics now,' Doc Craven interrupted, speaking for the first time. 'Get on, George.'

'Sure, Doc.... Wal, then we pulled a job which wasn't planned beforehand, there wasn't time. But it was the biggest yet, it was goin' to make us all rich. A drunk Wells Fargo agent talked big to Lafe in a hotel bar in Cheyenne, bragged about a parcel of uncut diamonds that he was helping to transport on a stage.

'We stuck up the stage an' we got the stones. It was as easy as that. There wasn't even a shot fired. But stones were something we hadn't handled before – it has allus been money or gold, stuff easy to use. At first, although he figured the worth of the stones as a hell of a lot, even Lafe didn't know how to convert 'em into cold cash. I wasn't in on his plans. I only learned what I did by listening, and listening good – most of the time when folks just didn't know I was listening.

'I listened to Lafe and Crane mostly, they were the clever ones. They thought first of taking the stones to 'Frisco, finding a fence there, But Crane said that was too risky, they'd either get themselves betrayed to the law or get themselves short-changed by some city slickers.

'Then Lafe thought about a man he used to know, that he'd met in 'Frisco in fact, but who wasn't there any more, had moved away for his health. His name was Jules Benton and Lafe had heard he'd founded a town way out in Montana and called it Benton City. Lafe said it was a real outlaw town and from there Jules had connections all over and, for a consideration, he'd handle the stones....'

George's voice tailed off. And Gabe Parker said dryly:

'Lafe was more than a mite behind the times. Jules Benton's been dead years an' Benton City's nothing like it used to be....'

'He knows that now, I guess,' said George. 'And is hopping mad about it. A man gets kind of out of touch laying in jail.'

'You didn't know about Jules either till you got here,' said Gabe. It was half-question half-statement. 'You hijacked the stones, figured you could beat Lafe an' the boys to it and get a price from Jules yourself. You took a hell of a risk both ways, my young friend. I knew Jules – he never backed the losing side and he would've figured you, a lone wolf, as a loser. He would've double-crossed you rather than have stacked up against a hellion like Lafe Bonarco.'

'I acted on the spur of the moment,' said George. 'An' I'll tell you why. I overheard the bunch talkin' about cutting me out, not giving me a fair share like always. They all seemed for it – even Lafe – all of 'em except Crane. Maybe it would've come to nothin'. I dunno. We'd got these rich stones but no money, no food except what we could steal. We were almost at each other's throats as it was.

'Still, I didn't want to finish one night with a knife in my back. So when the boys were sleeping off some rotgut booze they had stolen, I took a one-way *pasear*. I purposely hadn't taken much drink y'see. I took Lafe's body-belt, the stones. I threw the body-belt away....'

George spread his hands. 'I guess you know most of the rest.'

'You came into my shop to buy a gun. What happened to your own gun?'

'I dropped it, busted the firing pin. This was before I left the camp. Crane had it, was going to mend it for me. He's good with guns. He's a kind of gunsmith like yourself, I guess....'

'Did you leave your boots behind you?'

'Yes, I did, an' my saddle. All I had were moccasins – and a blanket.'

'You must've been loco.'

'Yeh,' said George. 'An' I didn't really want the trouble o' those goddamned stones I guess. I just took 'em for spite. If I'd had any sense I would've left anyway empty-handed, an' never laid eyes on Lafe an' the rest of 'em again....' George's face was becoming flushed. 'I'm sorry I....'

'That's enough,' put in Doc Crane sharply. 'You've talked too much. You've got to rest.'

'That's right.' Gabe Parker rose to his feet. 'I appreciate your telling me the whole story, George.'

The yellow-haired man lay back, his eyes half-closed. 'Maybe you've got a story to tell yourself, Mr Parker,' he said softly.

Gabe made no answer. The young man seemed to have depleted himself, was exhausted and half-asleep now. But as Gabe sauntered from the room he wondered what George Roddick had meant by that last remark, if he had meant anything at all, or had just been making conversation, delivering a rather lame parting quip.

Did George know the full circumstances of Gabe's early relationship with Lafe Bonarco? Did George know who Gabe Parker really was? Did it matter anyway? The way things were going, pretty soon everybody would know who Gabe Parker really was. Would it make any difference? Most of them had never heard of Gayelord Penrose, whose depredations, leading his notorious 'Coyotes' had occurred in the border states of Texas, Arizona, New Mexico, and had seldom reached as far back from there as Colorado, let alone distant Montana.

No, Gabe told himself as he bade Doc Craven 'so-long' ... no, it didn't matter much, except to him and his family and the few good friends he had in this now obscure community.

He felt an urge to vindicate himself.

Though he couldn't be sure – there were so many things about which he couldn't be sure. He figured that when approaching Benton City, Lafe Bonarco hadn't thought he would run into his old friend and mentor, Gay Penrose there.

Maybe the Fates had ordered all this, thought Gabe, maybe there was a pattern in life after all, maybe every man had a second chance. Maybe this was his: the chance to redeem himself, to partly right some of the wrongs he had done in the old days. Or, at least, to balance the scales more evenly, to clarify the pattern, leave it straight for those who came behind.

Gabe had pretty well worked out the yellow-haired man's movements subsequent to his leaving the gunsmith's yester-day. He hadn't told George of the death of Joe Gravez and wondered what George's reactions would have been if he had.

But the boy had some good stuff in him, Gabe had sensed this from the start. The boy was worth redeem-ing....

THIRTEEN

'MAKE YOUR PLAY!'

The boys were cold, hungry, unshaven and miserable. They were as viciously savage as a depleted pack of mangy wolves.

They were having to lie low longer than they had figured. The body of the old half-breed killed by Summer, had been found. Though, like Lafe had said, this couldn't be pinned on them, nobody had seen them with this old goat except the old goat himself, and he wasn't talking. Lafe's jokes, told in that unemotional voice of his, made the flesh crawl.

However – Gabby said there was so much sign near the scene of the old man's death that an army might have been marching and counter-marching there. Leastways, Gabby hadn't *actually* said all this: Crane had embellished the half-breed's taciturn gruntings.

Maybe, Lafe said, it had something to do with the hombre with the busted neck they had found on the trail before they caught up with the old man on his spavined mare.

Anyway, Lafe agreed, maybe it wasn't wise for strangers like them to be riding all over the territory large as life right now.

He figured that the old man, if he had the stones, had given them to somebody else before the boys caught up with them. And he had died to protect that somebody else, to give them plenty of time to get to Benton City. Where else in this godforsaken territory could they go but to Benton City?

So the boys would wait. But they couldn't wait too long. And in the meantime there was the problem of food.

That afternoon they topped a rise and looked down on the buildings of a small ranch or farm.

'Give me that spy-glass,' said Lafe.

Summer handed over the brass telescope, one of the things that had been packed on the back of the old man's spavined mare. Maybe it was going to come in useful after all. Lafe pressed the cold rim to his eye.

'Looks a rundown sort o' place,' he said.

Then: 'But wait a bit. Something's moving. *Somebody*. A little man – or maybe a kid.'

'Let me take a look,' said Crane and Lafe handed over the telescope.

After a bit Crane said, 'Yeh, looks like a kid.'

'Come on,' said Lafe and kneed his horse down the slope.

A small, lean figure met them in the littered yard, a shot-gun covering them steadily. A big hat and high-heeled boots and faded levis. But the male clothing did not disguise the form: the small high breasts striving against the thin cloth of the checkered shirt, the smooth hips, the slim waist.

'By all that's holy,' said Lafe. 'A woman.'

Summer guffawed. 'A pretty 'un too.'

She was indeed. Her hair was rammed under her wide-brimmed hat but auburn tendrils escaped here and there, brushing a smooth forehead and big clear eyes that looked fearlessly up at the four unshaven, travel-stained riders. Her sun-bronzed cheeks were full, her nose was just right, her lips were ripe but set in firm lines.

'She's got spunk,' said beanpole Crane, half to himself.

'What do you want?' she demanded.

Her voice was clear and high.

Summer guffawed again.

'Shut your trap,' said Lafe.

Summer buttoned up like a clam, sat his horse lumpishly, staring at the girl as if he'd like to eat her.

'You don't have to threaten us with no shotgun, miss,' said Lafe. 'We come in peace. We've rode a long ways an' we're hungry and thirsty. We wondered if you could give us a bite and a sup – in the name of hospitality.'

So Lafe aims to play it cool, thought Crane, and he was relieved. It was a pity that Lafe, with that voice of his, sounded pretty chilling even when he was acting friendly. Crane hoped the young lady didn't have any male kinfolk back in the house there who might get hornery.

The girl looked slowly and deliberately from one to the other of the four men while still keeping the shotgun levelled. She evidently wasn't too keen on what she saw. Her eyes rested on Crane and he gave her a courtly bow.

'We ain't much, young lady,' he said. 'Just saddle tramps. But we don't mean no harm.'

He saw that his frankness disarmed her a little. But she was canny. She kept the shotgun up. She handled it like a third arm and looked quite capable of using it if need be. A shotgun was a very deadly weapon. Crane didn't mean to argue with it. He figured Lafe was of the same mind too.

Summer would act as Lafe wanted him to act which right now was not to act at all. Which only left Gabby who slumped in his saddle like a filthy bundle of rags and looked half-asleep. Gabby was as treacherous and vicious as a loco sidewinder.

'Climb down,' said the girl. 'Take it easy.'

They did as they were told. Gabby got down last, almost falling from his horse.

'Is your paw at home, miss?' asked Lafe.

'My paw's dead. But my two brothers and our hand are out back. They're within hailing distance an' they carry shotguns like me. So don't try anything.'

'Ain't the little lady got a suspicious nature, Lafe?' said Summer.

Lafe glared at him. Summer closed up again, remembering perhaps how Lafe hated his name to be used in front of strangers. Many a man had been hanged because of a thing like that, he had once said.

The girl, though she still kept the shotgun levelled at them, seemed hesitant now. She said abruptly:

'Come into the kitchen.'

She made a motion with the shotgun, allowed them to precede her.

The kitchen, though cluttered and not over clean, was large and homely. They seated themselves at the long table of shaven logs. She put a huge pitcher of milk before them. Summer guffawed again but didn't say anything. He obviously didn't know what to make of this female. He was the sort who liked to frighten women. But this one didn't seem scared of him at all. She was such a slip of a thing too, though she did have all the bumps in the right places.

She put large earthenware beakers on the table and oatcakes and rich yellow butter and a plate filled with thick curly pink slices of ham.

The four men attacked the food wolfishly. Gabby in particular was animalistic in his guzzling. He finished first and rose. The girl reached for the shotgun which she had leaned against the wall beside her.

'Just go see horses,' grunted Gabby.

The door closed behind him. The girl held the shotgun, made as if to follow the half-breed, decided against the wisdom of this and subsided, leaning against the wall again. But she held on to the shotgun and, the way she was, she could cover the three men at the table and Gabby too when he came through the door again.

She was reassured by the sound of jingling bridles outside.

But when Gabby returned he came through the back door unexpectedly and took the shotgun from her. She swung at him and he grabbed her by the shoulder. Her shirt tore, revealing white flesh. He slammed her back against the wall.

'Nobody out back,' he grunted.

'They're not far,' blazed the girl.

But for the first time her voice trembled and there was fear in her eyes.

Gabby put the shotgun leisurely on the table, so that he could use both hands on the girl.

'Keep away from me, you filthy, stinking pig,' she screamed.

He cursed in bastardised Spanish and hit her sharply across the side of the face with his open hand.

'I tame you,' he grunted. 'I teach you say names.'

'You're a filthy, stinking pig like she says,' spoke up the voice of Crane. 'An' if you don't move away from her nice an' easy I'll blow a hole right through you…. Keep those hands clear, boy – keep 'em clear I say!'

Gabby backed slowly from the girl. He held his hands stiffly away from his sides as he turned to face the tall lean man who stood away from the table now, his drawn Colt levelled at the half-breed's middle.

'I kill you, Crane,' he said thickly.

'Get out of the line of fire, honey,' said Crane in his soft, Southern drawl.

With a little gasp the girl moved.

A flick of an emaciated wrist and Crane's gun was holstered again.

'All right then, you filthy, stinking pig,' said the tall gunfighter. 'Make your play.'

Summer half-rose in his seat. 'Sit down,' said Lafe, and the ape-man sat down again.

Lafe watched unemotionally the little tableau set before him; and he chewed rhythmically at the same time.

The two men faced each other in this pregnant moment of time. Gabby's swarthy face had paled so much that it looked yellow. The sweat lay upon it like a film of grease.

His eyes were mere black slits as evil as those of a rattlesnake poised to strike.

Crane's demeanour and features had not changed one whit. His face was always colourless; his eyes were pale too, the only difference in them now, and perhaps this was only noticed by the man facing him, was that they had gone strangely opaque. They were dead, pitiless: the eyes of a killer.

Crane stood relaxed, stooping a little as always. His long arms hung limply. He only wore one gun but he wore it low. His right hand, with the long, white prehensile fingers was never far from the scarred walnut butt. His pose was so negligent, however, that its very negative quality gave it an added menace that no amount of grimaces or threats could have surpassed.

Crane acted as if he didn't care whether he lived or died. And maybe he didn't.

On the other hand, Gabby almost seemed to vibrate with evil and the need for killing action. He was beside himself with hate and a terrible frustration. Something held his gun-hand as if in an invisible vice. He knew what he had to do. His heart and his brain and his guts told him what to do. But his limbs wouldn't obey the rest of him.

Deep in his half-Indian soul a kind of suspicion held him. He was afraid to die, afraid of the ever-after. But Crane wasn't afraid of death and a man who wasn't afraid of death was a strange and awful thing.

Slowly Gabby drew his hands further and further away from his sides, holding his palms outwards, revealing their empty helplessness. He let his head fall on his breast like a beaten cur.

'Apologise to the young lady, Gabby,' said Crane softly, in his gentle Southern drawl.

Gabby's head jerked up and his dull eyes flamed again. For a moment it seemed he would make a play after all. But he looked shiftily around him and did not act, did not speak.

'Do what the gentleman says, Gabby,' said Lafe Bonarco.

'Sorry,' mumbled Gabby and he turned, brushed past the girl and went through the door, leaving it swinging behind him.

'Watch him,' said Lafe to Summer and the big ape rose and shambled after the half-breed.

'I must apologise for my compadres, miss,' said Crane. 'They're a little uncouth.'

'He's right, miss,' said Lafe who, it seemed, had decided to play along with his lean friend and be a fine Texan gentleman.

'Thanks for the eat, miss,' he went on. 'Maybe we can repay you when next we pass this way.'

That voice, thought Crane – no life, no emotion, no human pity: everything he says sounds like a promise of evil.

Crane had a hard shell a mile thick but one thing he couldn't abide was misuse of women. He had been able to avert a very nasty incident. But he knew that that bloodthirsty half-Piute, Gabby, would take a chance to stick a knife in his back at the earliest opportunity.

The girl looked from one to the other of the two men. She did not thank Crane for what he had done, but her eyes were warmer when she glanced in his direction.

'Let's ride,' said Lafe.

He went over to the door. Gabby and Summer couldn't have been far away for he beckoned them and they were back in the kitchen within seconds.

Crane looked back as they breasted the rise. There was no sign of the girl. The rundown farm-buildings looked as dead as a fragment of a ghost town.

FOURTEEN

A DAY FOR
BURYIN'

There were two funerals in Benton City on that particular
day.

Young Burt Grogan was buried in the cool late of the afternoon. A real good time for a funeral, Grif Kallis said. Also it
gave the fat undertaker and the one-eyed lad who was his
assistant more time to prepare things. Old Sam Grogan
wanted his only son's last journey – the short one from the
undertaking parlour to the slopes of Boot Hill – to be a grand
one, a journey that the folks of Benton City would long
remember.

Sam wanted the full rig. Grif Kallis hadn't used the full rig
since Jules Benton died and had hardly expected he'd have
to use it again, though he had dreamed of doing so. It had
been stashed away in the back of the stables, gathering dust,
its plate glass sides flyblown, one of its ornate lamps shattered, its metalware tarnished and dirty, its padding sagging
and grimy.

Grif and his helper worked all night to get it in trim;

replacing broken glass, greasing, spitting, polishing, stitching. They worked by the light of flickering oil-lamps. They worked stripped to the waist. To a strange onlooker, somebody who didn't know Grif and the one-eyed youth, who was called Perce, this would have seemed like a scene from the depths of Hades.

The great yellow lard-body of Grif Kallis, roll upon roll of mountainous flesh, hairless and obscene. And the pear-shaped head to top it all and the sweat rolling over it all like dew down the mountain slopes.

And the pint-sized lath of a kid, Perce, a quick and white matchstick-man. A skinned bear and a skeletal sprite, solemn at first about their work on the grim black structure and then, when the woodwork and metal began to shine, doing a sort of ghoulish dance.

They took it in turn to have breakfast and a catnap. Then they worked through the morning, only taking a short break to bury Joe Gravez, the half-breed.

However, despite Grif's haste, it was surprising what a good funeral old Joe had himself after all.

Pretty well the whole of the population turned out. Even the local madam and her girls got up early to stare and giggle or, because it was customary with them, to weep a little with a lace handkerchief to the nostrils in a very ladylike manner. Maybe they didn't even know who the dead man was or, if they did, knew he had never been a customer of theirs.

But funerals weren't so frequent as they had been in the old days and only Big Lola, the madam herself, actually remembered the old days.

Anyway, this one would whet the appetite for the bigger show that was to come in the afternoon.

Even so, Joe Gravez's burying was a pretty good burying as buryings went.

For instance, it was a real old-type Western funeral.

There was no carriage. There were no horses, black or otherwise. The plain pine coffin was carried on the shoulders of six tall men of the community. Gabe Parker. Big Lon Staflen. Doc Craven. And three tall barflies who had known Joe vaguely and had certainly not looked down upon him. And, as it was still quite early, they were able to walk erectly and proudly bear their share of the burden.

... They had even made their separate vows to stay sober until after the second funeral, though they couldn't hope to take a hand in that and didn't particularly care to anyway. Joe Gravez had, like them, been a sort of misfit. He had been of their kind. But as far as they were concerned, old Sam Grogan, his dead son, his ranch and all his minions could be buried in a vast communal grave and they wouldn't turn a hair of their well-pickled heads.

Their names – these three – were Saul, Jeff and Bart, and if they had second handles nobody could remember them. This was their morning and they carried themselves with pride, helping Gabe, Big Lon and Doc to carry the burden and lead the cortege. And the rest of the mourners, with the Gravez family in the lead, pacing behind. Slow measured pacing – as far as the adults could manage. And the Gravez kids with their big sister, Maria, and Aunt Kate Parker and Aunt Prunella Parker; the kids forgetting their grief in their wonder of being in this, to them, marvellous big procession and all the people staring and nodding and the women calling them 'poor lambs' and other such things.

And the crocodile wending its way up the slopes of Boot Hill to the oblong hole in the ground and the wreaths and flowers piled around and the white-haired preacher waiting like God Himself.

Maria held herself erect and did not hide her face, though

the tears streamed slowly down her cheeks.

Papa would have been very proud of all this ... very proud.

Burt Grogan's funeral was a proud thing too, though in a different way.

Nobody in town had really liked Burt Grogan, no more than they liked old Sam and his boys with their big talk and their overbearing ways.

It was typical of old Sam to want a show, and the populace played along with him in that. But they spoiled it somewhat by streaming down Boot Hill afterwards and filling Benton City's three saloons (it was too early yet for the *other* places). Some of old Sam's boys joined them too, for though they could get along with the old man, who was a harsh but honest boss, they had disliked his lumpish son.

So what with all the festivities, and a few fairly harmless brawls and the girls chased and the bragging and the betting, nobody took much notice of the two strangers who drank first at one place, then at another, and kept their eyes open, but hooded and their mouths shut.

And if anybody took notice of these strangers they probably didn't connect them with two other strangers, dead ones, that Grif Kallis and Co. buried hastily that very night side by side in an unnamed hole on Boot Hill.

And then Grif, who had had quite enough burying for one day, went right home and to bed. And even his young assistant, Perce, was kind of worn and closed his other eye and went to sleep in the driving seat of the renovated hearse.

The two strangers – the live ones – were Crane and Summer, and they were studying the lie of the land before Lafe and Gabby moved in too.

Like Lafe had said, they'd leave that goddamned donkey (the mount Lolita, Joe Gravez's old mare) behind and the brass telescope too, and then nobody could tie them in with the killing of the old half-breed. Unless George Roddick did, of course.

Gabby had reconnoitred the adobe hut again and discovered that George had vanished. Lafe cursed himself: he had figured George was on his last legs. But obviously George had got some new strength from someplace, and he could be in Benton City now.

Still, even George couldn't prove anything about anything. Wasn't he an owlhooter himself? It would pay him to sing small unless he wanted to end on a lynch-rope – if Lafe and the boys didn't get to him first.

Lafe and Gabby made camp in a shrubbed and sheltered hollow some miles outside of town and they waited.

Lafe had purposely split up Gabby and Crane, sent the latter into town with the ape-like Summer. Lafe realised that the bad feeling between the lean Crane and the vicious half-Piute was only lying dormant and would flare up again if they weren't kept apart as much as possible. He needed both of them, if only as gunhands ... but, if worst came to the worst, he kind of hoped it wasn't Crane who got it in the neck.

Lafe was broke and hungry and savage and felt every now and then as if he had lost control of things completely. It was a new feeling to him and he didn't like it one little bit. The loss of the stones at the hands of a yellow-haired kid hardly out of diapers – this had really eaten into his guts. He had to get George and he had to get the one who had the stones – it hardly seemed conceivable that George still had them....

Most of all he had to get the stones. They were his vindication, his salvation, his only hope.

FIFTEEN

DEATH AT NIGHT

It was late when Crane and Summer rode back into camp.

The night was dark, with low clouds which obscured the moon, hid the stars. The atmosphere was sultry, making men and beasts uneasy. The very atmosphere seemed stretched to bursting point like an abscess waiting to release its poison.

The two men acknowledged Lafe's curt greeting; Gabby didn't speak at all but they were used to this. They hunkered down before the small fire and Lafe mechanically poured two cups of coffee and handed them over.

'Cripes,' said Summer. 'I'm dry. All we could afford was one drink apiece.'

'Yeh,' said Crane with a dry laugh. 'It's kind of embarrassing to hang about in a saloon without buying anything. There are only three places in Benton, luckily, none of 'em any great shakes and they were so packed with people busy celebrating the two funerals they had today that nobody took any notice of us.'

'Any talk?'

'About who killed the old man an' that?'

'Yeh.'

'Some. But not much. Folks seem to figure that whoever did it are to hell an' gone by now. Nobody 'ud expect the killers to show up in Benton City.' Crane laughed again. 'All those tough people there y'know! They're all deputy sheriffs now that that old marshal's laid up.'

'He ain't dead then?'

'Not last we heard.'

'Hear anything about George Roddick?'

'Nope.'

'What was the other funeral?'

'That young gink we found on the trail with a broken neck. Son of a big tinpot rancher hereabouts. His boys were throwing their weight about in town tonight. But they were already leaving when we came away.'

'So we'll move in come morning,' said Lafe.

'Seems a good idea,' agreed Crane.

Lafe looked at him morosely across the dying fire. Gabby sat hunched up Indian-like, his chin on his breast. He hadn't said anything.

'Ain't there anything to eat?' burst out Summer. 'I'm starved. They were giving food away in one o' those places tonight. Crane figured we better not take any, though, for fear o' drawin' attention to ourselves....'

'That was wise,' said Lafe.

'I'd like to take that town apart,' growled Summer.

He had had to sing small tonight and he didn't like that.

'Maybe you'll have your chance,' said Lafe softly and tonelessly. 'Maybe you will, ape.'

He sometimes called Summer 'ape'. If the lumpish man resented this, he didn't reveal the fact either by word or action, he was too scared of Lafe and his deadly fast gun.

But now he took out his spleen on Gabby, figuring no doubt that if Gabby started anything Lafe would stop it.

'You're the goddamned cook around here, dark man,' he said, 'where's the food?'

Gabby reached into the shadows just behind him and raked forth an opened can of beans. He held it in his hand and, though his eyes were hooded, revealing nothing, it seemed for a moment that he would fling the can across the fire at Summer.

But slowly he put the can down in the firelight, left it there.

The half-witted Summer was nonplussed. But finally he moved at a crouch around the fire and picked up the can. He also foraged round until he found the skillet, still greasy from Gabby and Lafe's own supper. He tipped the contents of the can in on top of this, scraping the residue out with his jack-knife. He balanced the skillet on top of the fire.

The four men sat looking at the skillet, listening to the fizzing fat, the popping beans.

They might have been the last four people left in a dark, dead world. Crouched in their little circle of firelight, their comfort, their meagre protection from the perils outside, they seemed so close and brotherly and compact, a team four-square against anything that slinked or prowled.

But the sultry night was like a blanket around them, press-ing in on them squeezing them, irritating them, building up a tension.

Summer, though rather unwittingly, had fanned Gabby's smouldering fury into a tiny flame that only needed a little more fuel to turn it into a wholesale conflagration, Or, least-ways, an explosion.

Gabby was superstitious and vicious and unpredictable. He was like some kind of night animal. Crane, for one, had known that if Gabby tried to get back at him for the insult he had put upon him at the tumbledown ranch the attempt would be at night. Crane figured that Gabby, having once backed away from a straightforward gunfight would not risk the same thing again. When his chance came Gabby would use a knife and he would try for one fatal blow – that was the sort of thing Crane decided he had to guard against.

To begin with, Crane was right in his surmise. In his half-Indian soul Gabby considered his honour was at stake, though had he been asked about this he wouldn't have used the word 'honour'; in fact, he probably wouldn't have been able to put the way he felt into words.

He only knew that he had to kill Crane. And, not having any ethics, hardly understanding the difference between right and wrong, he wasn't particular *how* he killed Crane, only that he succeeded in killing him very, very dead.

And Gabby didn't aim to get himself at all hurt in the process if he could possibly help it.

This was how Gabby had it figured, how he *felt* it – that is, until Summer started to rile him.

So, unwittingly, Summer, who usually had little to say to Gabby fanned the small flame and brought on the conflagration.

Though the actual flare-up, or explosion, came later that night and was not directed at Summer, it was directed at his saddle-pardner. At Gabby's own erstwhile pardner, now his enemy, beanpole Crane.

Crane and Summer ate their beans, spooning them from tin plates. They drank more hot coffee.

Both of them began to feel better. Summer put a bit more wood on the fire and the two men leaned back on their side of the flames.

Crane took out his little sack of 'makings' and handed them to Summer. The ape-like man muttered his thanks and rolled himself a smoke. His childlike mind had already forgotten how he had spoken to Gabby, had also forgotten the incident at the small ranch that afternoon.

Had Summer been in Gabby's place, had it been he that backed down before Crane, Summer would just as easily have forgotten that by now. He would not even have been ashamed of it at the time. He had no shame. He knew he was as fast with a gun as Crane or Lafe or Gabby. But he was the bully-boy when there was any beating-up to do and that pleased his pin-sized soul.

Crane offered his makings to Lafe but the latter declined with a shake of his head, a wave of his hand. Crane would probably have automatically offered them to Gabby. But Gabby seemed to be asleep. Asleep as an Indian sometimes sleeps, seated upright though slumped, tilted so far forward that, as he sat in this position, his face was completely hidden.

He was not asleep, however, and the thing that galvanised him into action was such a little thing.

Nothing was the way he had planned it. Though he had not planned anything really, had just decided to await his opportunity and then act swiftly and with the utmost deadliness.

But the hate spurted in him prematurely. The explosion came. He acted swiftly then … but prematurely.

It was such a little thing.…

Crane began to roll a smoke for himself. He wasn't normally a clumsy man, but, just then, he dropped his little sack of makings.

It fell in the hot ash at the rim of the fire.

Automatically Crane reached down and grabbed the sack. Then he swore violently as a fragment of redly-smouldering wood, the resin bubbling, became adhered to his hand.

He flicked it away and it fell on Gabby's knee, smouldered.

Such a little thing.…

Gabby's head jerked up so hard that his hat fell off. He

uncoiled, leapt to his feet, screaming in bastardised Spanish.

He went for his gun.

Crane was taken completely by surprise. But so highly-tuned were his reflexes that, even as Gabby's gun blasted, Crane was rolling.

The slug kicked up the ground an inch from his face. Gabby didn't have a chance to fire again.

At the end of his roll, while still in a reclining position, Crane drew; he fired from the hip.

The heavy slug hit Gabby in the shoulder, spinning him completely around. His gun did a parabola in the air, glinting momentarily before disappearing into the darkness. Gabby fell backwards into the fire and began to scream.

Crane fired again and Gabby shut up, jerked convulsively, then became still.

The night was filled with the odour of burning cloth.

Both Lafe and Summer were on their feet by now, though neither of them had drawn his gun. There was no need.

'Get him off there,' said Lafe tonelessly.

Summer bent, grabbed one of Gabby's arms and pulled him from the fire. His clothing was already alight, though he couldn't feel anything now.

Summer rolled the body over and over with his boot, until the flames were completely extinguished.

Summer stood looking down at the body. Gabby had never been much to look at and right now he appeared to be nothing more than a smouldering bundle of rags.

'Take him out there someplace an' bury him best you can,' said Lafe. 'Cover him anyway.'

He sat down again.

Summer and Crane looked at each other in the glow of the firelight. Then Crane shrugged.

'Catch hold of his legs,' he said.

Summer bent and did as he was told.

Crane grabbed the body under the armpits and they carried it away into the darkness.

Lafe watched them till they had disappeared. He spat into the dying fire.

When Summer and Crane returned, both brushing dirt from their hands, Lafe said:

'I guess it had to happen sooner or later. I wish it could've happened in another night or so though.'

'He asked for it,' said Crane softly. There was still a tenseness about him. His voice was thick.

'Yeh, I guess he did,' said Lafe. 'But it means one less for that town tomorrow.'

'Hell,' said Summer. 'What have *we* got to be scared of in a dead hole like that?'

Nobody answered him and he skirted the fire and wandered off into the darkness again.

His vague bulk was visible from time to time and the other two could hear him scribbling around, panting and grunting like a fat pig.

Finally he emerged into the firelight again, busily knocking the dirt and leaves from Gabby's gun which he finally tucked into his belt.

'Seein' as you're so goddamned busy you can kick some dirt on the fire,' said Lafe. 'We don't want anybody spotting us an' creeping up in the night.'

Guffawing as if this was the greatest joke in the world, Summer did as his master ordered.

Lafe and Crane began to lay out their bedrolls and pretty soon Summer joined them.

Another man had died.

All men die. So the living slept.

SIXTEEN

THE OWLHOOTER

That morning Gabe Parker made his sick calls again.

He first went to the marshal's office where, in the back room, Pete Bickerston lay abed. The old marshal was propped up against a mound of pillows. He looked more like his old self but, even so, wore a rather disgruntled expression, the reason for this being the lady who had elected to nurse him. Her name was Mrs Webber and she meant well, but she wasn't quite to old Pete's taste.

She was a twenty-stone widow with four kids and a heart appropriate to her size. She was the town's unofficial nurse and was partial to sick or wounded men with no attachments, age no object.

Widow Webber's husband had died in a gunfight during Benton City's 'roaring days'. The lady had been younger then, of course, and not so large, though past the buxom stage. She had needed a new man badly then but hadn't been able to capture one. Through the intervening years she had kept trying. She was still trying.

Pete Bickerston was a good twelve years her senior and had

been a widower for fifteen. He had no children and he loved his bachelor existence. Now, pinned to his bed, he had to suffer in silence widow Webber's blandishments and broth. She made mighty fine broth. But Pete would have given a gallon of it for a pint of good rye whiskey, a liquid from which he was temporarily banned by order of Doc Craven.

'Can't you get me out of here, Gabe?' he pleaded, after the beaming widow had left the room. 'Put me up at your place or somethin'.'

'I'm overloaded at my place already, you know that,' Gabe retorted. 'What with the Gravez kids an' all.'

'Oh, yeh. Sorry, Gabe, I forgot. What's goin' to happen to those kids anyway?'

'The town'll figure something out,' said Gabe. 'Folks are pretty good in a case like that, they'll turn up trumps. An' that girl, Maria, an' the eldest boy, José, are willing to work for the rest. They're a bright pair. They'll be all right.'

Pete Bickerston, though in his weakness he still craved drink, had since the shooting reached a new maturity. Gabe had already told him about Lafe Bonarco and his boys and George Roddick and the diamonds, the precious stones that were now in Gabe's own keeping.

Gabe said he figured that Lafe and his men had been responsible for Joe Gravez's death but he had no proof of this. He was pretty sure, however, that by now Lafe would have deduced that the stones were somewhere in Benton City. Pretty soon he would be leading his boys here. And nobody could touch them until they started something.

Pete had said that they were ultimately bound to start something in order to get what they came for. Pete wished he could get out of bed: he was the law in Benton City: he ought to be doing something.

He reiterated this statement now, but Gabe told him not to

worry. Then Gabe said So-long and left him.

He went from there to Doc Craven's surgery and home. This place was always 'open house' and Gabe passed through the half-open door. The waiting room was empty. Gabe crossed it, rapped on the upper glass panel of the doc's consulting room. There was no reply, so Gabe opened the door and walked in. Obviously Doc Craven was out on an early call.

Gabe crossed the consulting room and went through another door into the large cluttered living-room-cum-kitchen, redolent of a mixture of tobacco and the varied odours of its bachelor owner's profession.

The entrance to the stairs was in a curtained alcove at the right-hand side of the big room.

Gabe pushed aside the curtains and climbed the stairs to the small landing.

George Roddick was, or had been, in the room on the left-hand side. The door was closed now. In fact, both the doors on the landing were closed.

Gabe lifted the latch of the left-hand door, pushed the door open.

He opened his mouth to call, 'George', but the name died on his lips.

George Roddick sat up in bed, the Colt in his fist levelled steadily at Gabe's belly.

George Roddick's eyes were mere pale slits; his pale face was a set, expressionless killer's face.

Then slowly those eyes widened and the lean jaw sagged a little.

The gun was lowered too, and George grinned slowly a crooked, uncertain grin.

'Phew I nearly threw down on you, Mr Parker. I didn't hear you till you got to the door. You certainly move quietly.'

Gabe raised his hand, ran the fingers across his brow. They came away wet. 'I'll sing at the top o' my voice next time I come up here,' he said. 'Shocks like that ain't good for my old heart.'

'You're not so old – not the way you move.' There was an apology in George's voice, and a lot of respect too.

'I didn't learn to move like that just by being a gunsmith in a backwater like Benton City,' said Gabe soberly.

'I know that. The way you cut down Grimmond and Pales told me that. I only wish I'd been there to see it. Grimmond and Pales were a pair of skunks, but they were picked men. Lafe Bonarco picked 'em. And Lafe knows *how* to pick men! You knew Lafe, didn't you, Mr Parker, you said you knew him?'

The tone was diffident; but subtly inquisitive too.

'Yeh, I knew him,' said Gabe. He sat down in the basket-work chair by the bed.

'How've you bin, young George?' he asked.

'Oh, fine,' said George. 'Doc Craven's a good man, huh? A very good man.'

'A very good man,' agreed Gabe.

George stabbed a finger at the large, wicked-looking Colt .45 now lying on the bedclothes in front of him.

'He left this with me – the doc. He said, if anybody came up here an' bothered me I was to shoot 'em.'

Gabe grinned. 'I ain't bothering you, am I?'

'Not a a bit, Mr Parker.' George's eyes were bright now, birdlike, inquisitive.

But they quickly became hooded again and his voice was sober as he asked, 'Lafe and the boys will hit town soon, you know that, don't you?'

'I know that,' said Gabe Parker. 'We'll be ready for 'em.'

'You!' said George. 'They'll be after you. Whether they

116

know you've got the stones or not, they'll know you're a danger. You killed Grimmond and Pales. Yes, Lafe an' the boys'll be gunning for you. Who'll help you?'

'I've got friends.'

'You've got me,' said George. 'I'll get up when you want me. I can use a gun better than anybody else in this man's town – except you, I guess.'

'I guess.'

'I'm fast. I shoot straight.'

'You got a hole in your shoulder, your arm in a sling.'

'My *left* arm. I shoot with my right. Goddamn it, I can walk. Don't treat me as if I was a kid!'

'Easy … Easy,' said Gabe. 'I'll call you. I'll need you.'

'You promise!'

Gabe had never seen the yellow-haired younker so passionate. 'I promise,' he said softly. 'But first of all I want to tell you something an', after I've told you, maybe you won't want me to hold you to that promise. You might want to take it all back.…'

'Why would I?'

'The fight will be between me an' Lafe. It'll be a grudge fight. Forgetting the diamonds, forgetting everything and everybody else, it'll be just between me an' Lafe, a fight that's been building up an' brewing for many years. I guess both of us thought it would never really come, that we'd never see each other again. I guess we hoped we wouldn't. But it had to come, it was Fate I guess – or whatever you'd like to call it.

'Really, in the long run, the diamonds have nothing to do with it. Not the way Lafe is. Not the way I am. We were like brothers once. Like father and son – maybe not that: more like an uncle an' a favourite nephew, the uncle teaching the nephew all he knows and the nephew a willing pupil, striving

117

to emulate the uncle, then ultimately to beat him at his own game.'

Gabe paused. There was a faraway look in his eyes. As if to egg him on gently, George said:

'Once while we were in jail together, Lafe told me of a gang he used to ride with when he was younger. About my age I guess. They – this gang – useter call themselves the Coyotes. The leader was a man called Gayelord Penrose. Lafe referred to him as 'Gay'.'

'I'm Gayelord Penrose,' said Gabe.

'I'd begun to think that,' said George. 'Yeh, I guess I had.'

'Do you want to back out now?'

George shook his head. 'I never knew Gayelord Penrose. To me he's just a legend. I *know* Gabe Parker. I'll stick with Gabe Parker.

'Still,' he added. ''I'm as nosy as a cat in a cat mint patch an' if Gabe Parker wants to tell me about a certain small slice of his life I'll listen an' listen well. But what I hear ain't gonna change my viewpoint or my – er – decision in any way whatsoever.'

Gabe laughed out loud, the fullest and heartiest sound he had made since George had known him.

'Goshdurn it,' he said. 'What're you doin' here? With a gift o' the gab like you've got you ought to be in the Senate.'

But George, though there was still a half-smile on his lips, just looked at him and did not say anything else.

'All right,' said Gabe. But then he stopped again.

And George picked up the gun from the bedclothes in front of him; he raised it, pointed it at the door.

They listened to the footsteps on the stairs and waited.

Then the familiar voice of Doc Craven sang out, 'George.'

The young man put down the gun again. 'Come on, Doc,' he called. 'I'm having a pow-wow with an old friend of yourn.'

118

'Yeh, let's have the doc in on this too,' said Gabe. 'It's time I got something off my chest to one of my few very good friends in Benton City.'

'I was still just a kid when the war ended. But I had seen some hell. I had fought for the South in a Texas cavalry division. I hardly knew what the war was about. I only knew that I had to be in it. There was just pa' an' me. He was a gunsmith. A good one. Like him I've always loved good guns. Peacemakers, my pa always called them. It seemed funny, I suppose, that a man who spent his life with guns should be such a peaceful man. He didn't like the war. But he didn't object when I wanted to go. He knew what young men were.'

Gabe paused.

Went on:

'While I was away he got pneumonia and died. I couldn't get to him in time. When I finally got back home the war had finished and part of my home town was in ruins, my father's shop among them. I rode away from there and I never went back.

'I wore an old ragged Southern uniform and I was penniless. But my boots weren't bad and I had a good rifle and handgun and a pretty good horse. We'd travelled a long way together and we were to travel a lot further. I was riding the owlhoot trail when I finally lost that horse. He was shot by a lawman and I had to ride double with another man. We were lucky to get away.

'I had money in my pants by then though, plenty of it. I soon got another horse.

'I was still young. But I was old in the ways of owlhooters. I had ridden with some hard ones, some big ones. I had taken orders from some of the worst killers in the West. I was fast. I had always been fast. I realised that I didn't have to take orders from anybody, that I could give orders. I had a rep now and men would take my orders and follow me. That was when I started the Coyotes.'

Gabe looked at George. George nodded slightly and said nothing.

Gabe was still in the basketwork chair beside the bed. Doc Craven sat opposite him, on a hard chair titled back against the wall, his long legs stretched out in front of him.

He smiled thinly – he never grinned or laughed – and said:

'Hell, Gabe, are you telling me you used to be a bandit or something? Who hasn't? When the war was over half the young hellions who fought for the South carried on their own private war afterwards. They even wore their old uniforms – until they dropped to pieces. Folks in town have always thought there was some kind of a mystery about you, they've talked about you behind your back. In just the same way as they've talked about me – because we both chose to bury ourselves in Benton City. By now, since your exhibition of the art of self-defence here on their very main street everybody knows you're a gunfighter, that you must have been a "somebody" some time....'

'Is that how everybody measures "somebodies"?' said Gabe bitterly. 'By how fast they are with a gun, by how many men they have killed? Have I run halfway across the goddamned country just to come back to where I started from?'

The doc shrugged. 'That's life!'

'It is,' said Gabe, and he chuckled now. 'Why am I feeling so sorry for myself anyway. Let's end this little story....'

'Tell me how you met Lafe Bonarco?' said George.

'I'd met up with him a few times in different hideouts,' said Gabe. 'I'd ridden with him, I guess. But at first he was just a face. He was a kid, even younger than myself. Just a vicious kid. I'm not quit sure how he came to join up with me. It just happened.'

Gabe gave a little spurt of laughter. 'It seemed to me then that I was ages older than him but I guess I wasn't really....'

'You're not,' put in George Roddick. 'Not really.'

Gabe nodded, absently. He went on:

'I was his teacher. I taught him all the tricks. Soon he was almost as fast as I was. I guess he's faster still now....'

'He's fast all right. Can you take him, Mr Parker?'

'I can try.'

'There mayn't be any need,' said Doc Craven.

'I broke away finally,' said Gabe. 'I drifted out just the way I had drifted in. I'd wanted to be a big gunfighter, a leader. Then suddenly I didn't want to be either of these any more. The Coyotes got another leader, Lafe. And I moved on and on. I kept on moving. But my rep kept catching up with me. I had to keep defending myself against tough gunnies who wanted to take over – each one wanted to bear the rep of having been the one who killed Gayelord Penrose. I had to kill in self-defence. It was kill or be killed. And I was sick of killing.

'I met Kate and married her and we had Prunella and I changed my name and we kept on moving.'

Gabe spread his hands. He was looking at Doc Craven now. 'The rest of it I guess you know.'

'So you became a gunsmith like your father,' said the doc. 'And you finally settled in Benton City. You could've just as easily become sheriff or marshal of Benton City. Many gunfighters did become lawmen, began to fight for the law instead of against it. Times have changed, Gabe. The past is buried.'

'Part of it, doc. Only part of it.'

'So?' Doc shrugged. 'That's life,' he said for the second time.

He rose. 'I guess I've got some patients waiting now.'

He left the room.

And, not long after, Gabe followed him.

Gabe was outside the doc's place when he saw Lafe Bonarco and two other men dismount at the hitching rack down the street and enter Benton City's largest saloon, the Seven Spot.

Everything was following a pattern it seemed.

It was Fate maybe. Inevitably. As if ordained.

The past was never quite buried....

SEVENTEEN

APE ON THE LOOSE

Propping up the bar at the Seven Spot Saloon when Lafe and the boys entered were three tall men.

They were, respectively, counting from left to right, Saul, Jeff and Bart.

They were the three barflies who, together with Gabe Parker, Lon Staflen and Doc Craven had, in the old-style Western funeral of yesterday carried the coffin that contained the mortal remains of old Joe Gravez.

Yesterday had been their day of days. They had walked proudly and erect, bearing their burden well. They had relived that moment since, over and over again. Last night free drinks had been theirs. All three of them were practised spongers, but last night they hadn't needed to sponge.

Last night the Seven Spot had been packed. It had been literally jumping. Booze had run like water. Free booze. Even old Sam Grogan's boys had been affable and generous. None of them had been grieving about the death of the boss's son. It might even have been thought that they were celebrating. Grieve, celebrate, what-you-will – for free booze Saul, Jeff and

123

Bart would stand on their heads. If they were sober enough to do so.

But now the morning-after was here – with a vengeance. Saul, Jeff and Bart felt as if they had been standing on their heads for weeks. The effects were pretty awful. Saul, Jeff and Bart propped up the bar in the Seven Spot – which was nearly empty – and sipped, actually *sipped*, at the one drink apiece that had been donated to them by the barman. They strove to stay erect, if not as proudly as yesterday; they strove to prevent their respective heads from bouncing from their necks and hitting the ceiling.

They managed to turn those heads enough to survey the three newcomers when they entered the saloon. But then they turned them back; so quickly that they emitted a soft chorus of groans. The three strangers were hardcases and they were dirty and ragged, kind of beat-up looking. They definitely weren't the sort to be doling out free drinks.

Saul, Jeff and Bart would have been surprised had they known that right now one of the strangers was talking about them.

Crane said: 'Those three at the bar, those three soaks, they were in here last night doin' a lot of jabbering. Seems like they were bearers at Joe Gravez's funeral. Me and Gabby tried to get near to them but it wasn't any use and, like I've said before, right then we didn't want to draw undue attention to ourselves. Anyway, by the time Gabby an' me became aware of 'em those three galoots weren't making much sense anyway.'

'They look as if they'd talk now if their tongues were lubricated,' said Lafe.

'An' what do we do for spare money?'

'I got a mite in my belt I was keepin' for a rainy day.' After a fair amount of minor contortions Lafe produced a tiny wad of folded greenbacks.

'I swear!' said Summer.

The barman was at hand. Lafe called for drinks. He pointed to the three men along the bar.

'Those three fellahs look kinda lonesome and sad. Will you ask 'em if they'll do us the honour of having a drink with us. And will you bring them over to the table over there?' Lafe jerked a thumb at a table in a far corner, a large expanse of floor all around it. It was an ideal place for exchanging confidences.

The barman blinked. These three hellions were the queerest Santa Clauses he had ever seen. But he knew Saul, Jeff and Bart weren't particular. So he did as he had been told.

And almost before he had got his message completely over to them the three barflies had joined the three strangers at the corner table.

After the first few rounds of drinks it was like old home night over there.

Saul, Jeff and Bart were talking their heads off. All it needed to keep them going was a cunningly-worded interjection from time to time from Lafe or Crane.

Though the three gabby, good-natured, rye-pickled barflies didn't realise it, their tales about the folks in and around Benton City were building up a lot of several kinds of hell for that fair community.

The three newcomers got accommodation in the only establishment in town that had the right to call itself a 'hotel'. All the rest were just boarding-houses or common shakedown establishments of the simplest kind. And nobody would dream of putting the cribs in the red-light district – a mere corner of town – in the hotel category.

There was a minor convention of drummers in town. Benton City was a stopping-off place for these fast-talking peddlers of various commodities. Accommodation was limited. Lafe and Crane got to share a small room with a double bed and Summer had to be content with an attic which hardly gave him space to stand upright.

At this stage of the game the three boys didn't like being separated. But there seemed little alternative.

Anyway – as Lafe said – Summer had taken quite a drop to drink and would probably go up those narrow dusty stairs and sleep like a pig.

And in the meantime Lafe and Crane took time out to chew over the information they had received from the three barflies.

'The way I figure it,' Lafe was saying. 'The old half-breed gave the stones to his daughter an' then led us off so that she and the kids could reach Benton City.'

'Yeh,' said Crane. 'He made himself a sitting duck – a dumb duck. An' now the stones are in the possession of that old compadre of yours, Gay or Gabe or whatever you call him.'

'I'd like to bank on that,' said Lafe. 'An' those half-breed kids are there too at the gunsmith's shop. Maybe those kids can be Gay's weak spot.'

'I get your drift.'

'What I can't figure though,' said Lafe, going off at a tangent, 'is what's happening to George Roddick. If he got to town, it's funny those three souses didn't get to know about it. They seem to have known about everything else.'

'Yeh, I guess we pumped 'em dry all right. Maybe George wandered away and died in a corner someplace.'

'So we'll forget George. Time to think about him an' take care of him if he does come back from the dead all of a sudden.' Lafe wasn't trying to be funny. He rose from his seat on the edge of the bed.

'Hell, I feel as if my throat's cut,' he said. 'I wonder if we can get some eats in this hole.'

'Maybe it'd be better to have it up here anyway.'

'Maybe you're right.'

'All right. You sit tight. Give me a couple of those green-backs you've got left an' I'll go see what I can rustle up.'

Lafe handed over the money and Crane left the room.

Downstairs he managed to get beef sandwiches and a couple of bottles of beer. He didn't see Summer around. He figured the ape was sleeping, decided against getting him some sandwiches too. The ape had been told to stay in his room.

This was one time, however, though Crane didn't know it, that the ape got some ideas of his own.

He did sleep, but not for long. When he awoke the light was fading. His tiny attic was full of smokey greyness that reminded him of his cell back at Yuma State Penitentiary. The memory was unpleasant. He suddenly felt in need of company. He was also pretty hungry, and dying for a drink.

Right then he didn't feel like calling in on his old cell-mate, Lafe, and the lanky Crane. They might not think it a good idea his going out on a foraging expedition on his lone-some. So he half-crept down his own narrow flight of stairs and passed their door, hearing the faint murmur of their voices and went on down the second flight.

He had a thick head and he felt mean, despising this one-horse burg and everybody in it.

He was spoiling for trouble.

Undertaker Grif Kallis and hostler Barnaby Jimson, both single men, always took their early supper in the hotel dining room, before adjourning to the Seven Spot Saloon for some serious drinking. They always sat at the same table near the arched and curtained entrance and they were the first to see

Summer enter that evening.

He was a stranger, and a pretty mean-looking one too, consequently they stared. He gave them an evil look, seated himself at an empty table further in the room and banged on it with his fist for attention.

A small, dark-skinned girl with a plump, curvaceous body and a pretty face came forward to him. Though Summer did not know it this was Maria, the daughter of the old half-breed he had killed only yesterday.

Maria, wanting to start in right away repaying the towns-people for their unwonted kindness had elected to work in the hotel that evening in place of the regular girl, who had croup. Gabe Parker had been reluctant to let her leave the house, but she had been so insistent that he had temporised, resolving that he or one of the other of his friends would arrange to be near her all the time.

Consequently, here were Grif and Barnaby – who would have been here about this time in any case. And in a little while Gabe himself would take their place.

'A steak,' bellowed Summer. 'Thick as this.' He made a measurement with his thumb and forefinger. 'An' some wheat cakes an' hot syrup and plenty of coffee, hot an' black an' sweet. An' make it fast, huh, my pretty one!'

He saw the startled look in the girl's big dark eyes and he threw back his head and guffawed. That was the kind of look he liked to see. She wasn't a bad-looking piece either. Kind of young. But plump and wholesome, just the way he liked them.

Maria fled. He took another good look at her before she disappeared in the kitchen. Plump as a partridge. He guffawed the louder.

At their table Grif and Barnaby exchanged glances. A dumb one. But a mean one too, who could be pretty dangerous. Shoulders like the end of a barn and a chest like a roof. Wearing a gun low, as if he could be fast, even though with all that bulk he didn't look it.

Summer tailed off into a spate of grunting giggles then looked around him as if awaiting comment. Nobody said anything. Everybody, though not without trepidation, awaited what would happen next. The way this stranger looked, something else was just *bound* to happen.

A few of them could not stand the suspense, however, and sidled out before the girl came back.

In just the same way they had made themselves scarce when a booze-soaked old man with a badge faced a killer on the street a few short days ago.

But Grif Kallis and Barnaby Jimson stayed put.

Gabe Parker had told them that maybe Maria had some idea about the men who killed her father and that they might want to shut her mouth for good. Gabe hadn't thought it wise to tell anybody yet about the uncut diamonds, the real reason why those killers, having put two and two together, might come after the girl.

But Grif and Barnaby had believed the half-truth that Gabe did tell them, so here they were, watching and waiting.

And finally Maria returned, carried her steaming tray across to the stranger's table.

Summer didn't say anything to her this time. Not at first. He didn't emit another of his explosive guffaws, didn't even grin. Just sat back and watched her with his evil black shoe-button eyes, his mouth half-open as if he was drooling, revealing yellow stumps of teeth.

He hadn't bothered to shave lately, hadn't even bothered to wash. Not for him the fancy ways of Lafe and Crane. These things were something they just couldn't make him do and as they themselves were unshaven and travel-stained much of the time, they didn't press him.

To the girl he looked fearsome. He even *smelled* fearsome. Like a dirty half-loco grizzly bear. He made her shake inwardly with the superstition that, though she might fight it, was still deeply ingrained on her half-Indian soul. Maybe deep down there too she suspected that this man, this monster, had had something to do with her father's death.

She tried not to get too close to him as she placed out the food on his table. He sat motionless and she could feel his eyes roving over her body as she moved.

But finally she had finished her task and she turned away.

He grabbed her round the waist. She was pulled down forcibly on his knee.

'Feed me, honey,' he bellowed. 'Come on, feed me!'

She struggled, but she didn't stand a chance against his ape-like strength.

Grif and Barnaby both rose to their feet.

And it was then that, behind them, Gabe Parker entered the room.

EIGHTEEN

THE FIGHT

Grif and Barnaby did not see Gabe enter. He went past them with what seemed incredible speed. They were, in fact, not completely aware of him until he reached the big fellow, grabbed him.

Then they stopped dead, awaited the speed of development, ready to step forward again if they were needed.

Summer had both of his arms firmly around the girl's waist when Gabe's hands fell on him, one on each shoulder, gripping like twin steel claws.

'Let the girl go,' said a voice in his ear.

It was not loud, but it was thick and vibrating with fury.

Involuntarily, Summer's grip on the girl slackened and she twisted away, ran, turned at a safe distance.

Summer felt himself being jerked to his feet. He was spun around. Then a fist that felt like a rock slammed full into the centre of his face, mashing nose and lips sickeningly. And he was propelled backwards, his heels rucking and grooving the threadbare carpet.

He lost balance completely, his hands flailing the air. He

131

hit a table with the small of his back. A leg snapped; the table collapsed beneath his weight; luckily there was nobody sitting at it. Summer found himself sprawling in a tangle of wood, his head singing as if a hive of bees had been let loose within it. Blood ran down his chin from busted lips.

However, he was tougher than hickory and, although his face ached, he was actually more shocked than hurt. He was a seasoned brawler, always depending on sheer weight and brute force in order to beat his opponent. Truth was, though, that lately he hadn't had many opponents, only victims.

His little piggy eyes became focused on the man who stood there in front of him. He blinked. The man was big, but not as big as Summer himself. He was older than Summer too: there were wings of grey in his black hair. But what made Summer boggle most of all was that beneath his short black walking coat the man wore a dirty white apron tied at the waist by a string.

What was this – a goddamned grocer or something?

Summer threw back his head and bellowed with laughter. It was not only that he was surprised and amused at the look of this man, but he had always found that his jeering guffaw made people mad, reckless, made them easier meat.

This hombre was heavy, he had flung quite a punch. But he was no *fighter*. Just look at him, standing there patiently, waiting.

He waited until Summer's mirth had subsided, then he said in that quiet, hard voice:

'Get up, you grinning ape, before I kick your face in.'

Summer blinked again. He looked about him quickly. Many of them had taken their chairs away. The dark young girl who had been the innocent cause of the fracas stood wide-eyed in the kitchen door.

Summer guffawed again, gathered his feet under him and

leapt upwards and forward like a human battering ram.

He was a damsight faster than he looked. Gabe Parker side-stepped quickly, but still Summer's elbow caught him in the side as the ape went hurtling past. Gabe was buffeted sideways, had to grab the edge of the table to prevent himself from falling. He felt as if he'd had a sly kick in the ribs from a fractious mule. Also he had been knocked too far out of line to deliver another blow at the big man as he blundered by.

He circled, backed a little. Another table had brought Summer to a stop, holding him this time, though its contents of plates, glasses and cutlery were swept to the floor in hideous cacophony. Summer twisted, found his opponent facing him again. Summer was not so precipitate this time. Even in his pinpoint brain he realised now that this white-aproned man was no amateur, as he had first thought. He moved with the speed and litheness of a professional.

Had the ape but known it, his opponent had learned his rough and tumble fighting in one of the hardest schools in the States, if not in the world: the Barbary coast.

In his youth, before the war, the footloose Gayelord Penrose, breaking away from stultifying family ties, had worked as a stevedore and roustabout on the docks. He had fought with the best of the batterers and gougers and biters, men who thought nothing of thumbing out a man's eyeball, chewing the ears off, or kicking his head to pulp with steel-tipped boots. He had had a few refresher lessons too when, years later, he hit Benton City for the first time and fell foul of various of Jules Benton's hardcases, many of these trained in 'Frisco too.

The two men watched each other warily.

'Come on an' fight,' growled Summer. 'What are you waitin' for? Are you yeller?' He punctuated the questions with several mouthfuls of filth.

Gabe Parker smiled, thin-lipped. The grey, abysmal cold-ness of his eyes did not change. He reached forward with one hand and crooked his forefinger.

'Come on, ape,' he said softly. 'Come on now, ape. Come on.'

Why did everybody call him 'ape'? He didn't like it! Summer launched himself forward once more.

Gabe placed one foot forward, set himself; he hit Summer once more, full in his already puffed and bleeding face. The impact was so hard, travelling bone meeting more bone, that Gabe thought his wrist would snap or his shoulder become dislocated. But Summer left him again, was propelled back-wards, skittling a table.

Somebody cheered softly and gleefully. It may have been Barnaby Jimson.

People ranged the walls. Some of the more bold were sitting down. The word had got around, and more people came in.

The hotel proprietor, peglegged Carl Rimmer, had hastened downstairs to see what all the commotion was about. At first he wished he had brought his gun. Then when he realised one of the fighters was Gabe Parker he wasn't so peeved. He knew Gabe would make good any damage to furniture, utensils and etceteras. Also Carl who had lost his leg fighting sharks in the Pacific, had seen Gabe in action years ago. It was a sight that would be well worth seeing again. Carl found himself a chair and, ignoring surprised glances, chose himself a grandstand seat.

'Vun for hiss knob, Gabe,' he said, and chuckled gleefully.

Summer's face streamed with blood as he clambered to his feet again. He brushed his eyes with his fist, dappling blood on his forehead too. He was a fearsome sight and the girl he

134

had handled crossed herself and murmured a quick prayer in Spanish.

Summer's shirt was torn at the elbow. A strip of it wreathed his lower arm. He tore it away savagely. He tossed it petulantly in the direction of Gabe Parker. Somebody laughed nervously. Summer glanced around him, snorting through his battered nose like a goaded bull. He couldn't remember anybody making a fool of him like this before. Maybe he didn't feel he was a fool. But in his pint-sized mind he was beginning to realise that he had sold this aproned man very short.

And now, as if to bear out this, Gabe Parker took off his coat and revealed his rolled shirtsleeves and muscular arms. The wide sloping fighter's shoulders, stooped now in a half-crouch, the hands half-clawed, the feet spread in the stance of a seasoned brawler.

He had stopped playing around now. He had had all Lafe's pardners described to him by George Roddick and now he realised that this must be one of them, could quite easily be the one who had killed Joe Gravez.

But don't go off half-cocked, Gabe, he told himself – remember this one is indeed a killer, an ape. Less intelligent than an ape in fact, a human chopping block who would not give up until he was beaten into oblivion.

NINETEEN

THE LESSON

Crane went out on to the landing, then returned.

'There's something going on downstairs,' he said. 'Sounds like a fight.'

Lafe smiled thinly. 'The townsfolk are probably celebrating our arrival.'

Crane said, 'I wonder ...' Then he broke off.

He sat down. Then he rose again. 'I'll go see if Summer is still snoring.' Before Lafe could say anything to this, Crane left the room.

He climbed the stairs soundlessly on long legs. It was dark now, but he went unerringly like a cat. The landing at the top of the stairs was tiny. There was only one door and this was closed. No sound issued from behind it, no tremendous snores.

Crane opened the door, stepped inside. Right away he knew the place was empty.

He took the stairs two at a time and burst in on Lafe. The latter, jumping up, almost drew his gun.

'Summer's not there.'

136

'Come on.' Lafe shouldered past Crane, led the way.

He slowed himself a bit when he reached the bottom of the stairs. He smiled, tried to look as pleasant as he could. The lamplight fell on his bare head, the thick black hair with its jagged streak of silver.

The small hotel lobby was thronged. People were pushing to the entrance of the dining-room. The curtains were parted; people were clustered at the doorless arch.

The two men split a little, wended their way forward. Crane was very polite, a real Southern-type gentleman. Lafe did his best. They had both cleaned themselves up, but they still looked hard and dangerous, had *lobo* written all over them.

People gave way to them, instinctively, after a quick side-long glance. Pretty soon they were at the archway and could see into the dining-room

Summer was there all right.

The two fighters had got past the feeling-out stage and, judging by the condition of Summer's face, he had got the worst of it.

By now his shirt was almost torn from his back. Blood oozed from a livid scratch amid the curly black hair on his chest.

His opponent had one eye closed and was bleeding gently from the nose. His shirt was split open down the front, but the tied apron held it intact. The white apron was speckled with blood.

'Gay Penrose,' breathed Lafe in Crane's ear.

'So that's the legendary Gayelord,' said Crane softly.

'Yes,' he mused. 'He has a certain look about him, even in that apron. I wonder how Summer managed to tangle with him.'

'I'll kill that ape,' said Lafe.

'You may not need to.'

'Gay's good. But he won't stop Summer.'

'He's having a dam' good try.'

'Summer can go on forever…. I wonder if the goddamned ape blew his mouth. I wonder how this started.'

A face appeared between the two men. It was a vapid unshaven one belonging to one of the barflies who had been bosom buddies with them early today, the one called Bart.

'Hallo, friends,' the face said.

Crane glanced about him. The other two, Saul and Jeff were nowhere in sight. Maybe they were still sleeping off their free binge.

'Howdy, pardner,' said Crane affably. He jerked a thumb in the direction of the circling fighters. 'What started this?'

'The big stranger insulted the young Gravez girl, Maria, the one I told you about whose Paw was killed. Look, there she is, over by the kitchen door.'

Crane nudged Lafe. But Lafe's eyes were already fixed on the plump, dark young girl. Pale killer's eyes, staring with a frightful intensity.

But he couldn't get at her because the fighters were clashing again.

They were both slower. They swapped blows in the centre of the room, wielding their fists like hammers. Some of the blows connected, dully. Others missed. Around them was the wreckage of furniture and crockery. The rich steak that Summer had ordered was trodden into the rutted carpet.

Gabe Parker slipped, half-fell. Summer aimed a kick at his face. It missed, grazed Gabe's shoulder. Gabe got up with a blow that sank into Summer's wide middle. The giant grunted, doubled. Gabe jerked up his knee. It hit Summer's jaw with a crack, jerking him upwards and backwards.

Gabe Parker went after his man.

Summer rolled, kicked out once more, this time from a half-reclining position.

Gabe side-stepped in time but tripped over a broken chair. Then it was his turn to roll on the floor.

There was nothing pretty about the fight. It was gruelling. It was mauling.

The two men faced each other again. They circled, moved in, clashed. Then used everything they had now. Feet, fists, elbows, hands. Every dirty trick they had learned in street-fighting. Between the two of them, that was considerable.

They wrestled now. Summer threw Gabe, then dived at him knees forward, seeking to crash the cage of his ribs. Gabe rolled. Summer half-fell across him, hands gouging for his eyes. Gabe chopped outwards with the edge of his hand. Missed Summer's adam's apple, but delivered a cutting blow to the side of his neck. Summer went backwards, feet flailing. Gabe grunted audibly as one of his opponent's heavy boots caught him in his already battered ribs.

He squirmed to his feet. But Summer was almost as quick. In Gabe's wake, he grabbed at Gabe's ankle. Gabe kicked out at him. The heel of his boot connected with Summer's jaw with a dull crack. Summer let go. But he was on his feet again as quickly as Gabe.

This ape seemed to be made of iron.

They circled. Their positions had changed now. They were near the window, leaving their arena behind them.

Gabe adopted a half-crouching, fighting-cum-boxing stance now. He guarded. He feinted. Summer tried him with a roundhouse swing and missed. Gabe moved in and under. He punished the giant's middle with rapid blows, he drew off, measured his man, let go. A straight-arm jab to the point of the jaw, all the strength of his powerful shoulders behind it.

Summer went back through the window in a terrible

cacophony of breaking glass, taking part of the frame with him.

'You go downstairs and wait,' said George Roddick. 'And I'll get dressed an' walk you home.'

'Oh no, you mustn't,' said Prunella Parker. She finished. 'You're not well enough.'

'Except for this arm I'm as well as I'll ever be.' He grinned.

He made a motion to get out of bed and the girl fled.

'Don't you dare go without me,' he yelled.

'All right.' The reply came floating back to him.

He got out of bed, tested his pins for strength, began to dress.

The small tub of calves-foot jelly the girl had brought him lay on the small bedside cabinet.

She was a sweet girl. He wished he had met her earlier. A girl like that could have set him straight years ago.

He grinned to himself. What was he, ninety or something? There was still time. Then his face sobered again, his thoughts with it. How much time *did* he have?

If he could settle in Benton City with a girl like that. With *that* very girl! If she'd have him. If. *If....*

The shadow of Lafe Bonarco loomed in his mind, assuming gigantic proportions.

He was glad to descend the stairs, not forgetting to tuck his gun into his belt before he left his room.

Prunella was chatting to the doc as she waited. The lamplight fetched chestnut glints from her dark hair. George thought he had never seen such a picture. He didn't want to leave it, didn't want to go out into the dark street. And this was not because he was afraid.

He realised Prunella's folks would be worried if he kept her too long.

'Are your ready, my lady?' he said, trying to make a courtly bow the way he used to see Crane do it.

The girl rose, smiling. 'Yes, I'm ready.'

George expected the doc to say something about his getting up without permission. But the doc just smiled, said, 'Don't do any fancy gallivanting, I want you back here, pronto.'

'Yes, suh.'

George took the girl gently by the arm and led her away. Doc Craven watched them go, a little enviously, a little tiredly, even a little sadly. They seemed well-matched those two. But could they ever make a go of it, he wondered.

The objects of his reflection closed the outer door behind them and made their way slowly along the boardwalk.

Light streamed from the hotel nearby and they heard the commotion before they got to it. People were hurrying to the hotel, climbing the steps. Prunella and George heard a man shout something about 'a fight'.

'Let's cross the street,' said George.

'I'm not made of paper,' said the girl tartly. 'The town was a lot rougher than this when we first came and I was only a kid.' But there was a half-chuckle in her voice.

'I didn't mean that,' George hastened to say. 'I just mean....'

He floundered. He gave up trying to explain what he *had* meant: he wasn't quite sure himself. He only knew that he considered this beautiful girl at his side to be a real lady, and that he wanted to protect her from anything unpleasant.

But they were abreast of the hotel now, though they had stepped into the street to avoid the knot of people that were gathered there on the sidewalk.

It was then that Summer came flying through the window, spraying glass, bringing part of the wooden frame with him.

141

The people broke in all directions in panicky fragments. Even Prunella and George backed involuntarily, though they were further away. George's hand dropped to the butt of his gun, stayed there.

'By all that's holy, it's Summer,' said George.

'You know him?'

'Yes.'

Things happened very quickly then. And terribly. George was sorry Prunella had to see it.

The boardwalk sagged beneath the impact of Summer's heavy body. He rolled off the edge of it, rolled beneath the hitching rail and between a pair of horses that were tethered there.

Both beasts were already restive, startled by the noise of breaking glass, the thudding and the creaking. Then this thing rolling between them was the last straw. They began to kick.

Summer wasn't quite unconscious and he began to scream hoarsely.

There was the sound of hooves striking home on flesh and bone. Summer was pinned, pulverised. There was one final thud, a sickening one like a smashing of a huge eggshell.

And the man became still, silent.

Lafe and Crane had not bothered to run outside with the rest and see what had happened.

'A lesson in how to tame apes,' said Crane.

'Never mind that now,' said Lafe. 'Let's get that Gravez kid.'

They looked about them warily.

Gabe Parker had not seen them, was already climbing out of the window in the wake of Summer, though it was pretty certain that the fight was over.

Other people were clustering behind Gabe, peering, craning.

Others were going in the opposite direction, running across the hotel lobby to the main floor and the street. Among them was peg-legged Carl Rimmer, the hotel proprietor.

The centre of the dining-room was empty except for scattered wreckage.

The plump, dark girl had fled.

TWENTY

VENGEANCE RIDE

They caught Maria as she was halfway across the kitchen. Hand over her mouth, Lafe dragged her into the alley which ran beside the hotel. The horses were round back, ready for a quick getaway.

Crane stayed at the kitchen door, his gun menacing the fat negro cook, the simpleton odd-job man and a squealing elderly woman whose function there was indeterminate. Crane waited for Lafe's whistle, the old Coyote signal, which would tell him everything was all right, get out there, ready to ride, to shoot if need be....

But, in this case, Crane did not wait for the whistled signal.

He saw a man pass the kitchen door, moving in from the street, going after Lafe.

Crane hissed at the three cowed people. 'Any of you move a muscle and I'll start blasting.'

They were petrified. They didn't mean to move.

Crane stepped into the alley.

A familiar voice said: 'Let the girl go, Lafe.'

George Roddick, limmed in the glow from the kitchen,

144

had his back to Crane. His left arm was in a sling. In his right hand he held a gun which pointed at Lafe, who had turned to face him, was holding the Gravez girl in front of him as a sort of half-shield.

Crane stepped up behind. Some sixth sense warned the young man and he started to turn.

Crane laid the barrel of his gun neatly but forcibly across the top of George's head. George crumpled to the ground with a little sigh, his Colt falling in the dust before him.

Lafe had his own gun out now, which meant he only held the girl with one arm. She twisted desperately, flung up her hand, raked at the man's face with sharp nails. Lafe let go. He staggered backwards, cursing. The girl ran, neatly eluding Crane.

There was a cry from the end of the alley. Both Crane and Lafe saw the other form there, taller and slimmer than the Gravez kid. The two girls running towards each other in anxiety, caught momentarily in the light from the kitchen window and the half-open door. The smaller one running away, the other one so patently running towards the man on the ground, unafraid of the two gunmen there.

'Let's get out of here,' said Crane.

They mounted their conveniently-placed horses. They rode away into the blackness of the arid plain behind the town and they were not chased.

'Why didn't you kill him?' panted Lafe.

'I've never shot a man in the back,' said Crane, 'and I don't aim to start now. Besides,' he added. 'A shot would have brought the whole town about our ears.'

'You could've killed him.'

'Hell, there wasn't time!' Crane sounded unusually pettish. 'He was out cold, no more trouble to us. You ought to've held on to the girl.'

Lafe didn't take him up on this; only said: 'We'll get all of 'em yet,' though it was not quite clear who, *or what*, he meant.

Back in the alley the two girls paused, together for a fraction of time, wordlessly. Then Maria turned about, joined her friend, Prunella. And they both went to George Roddick, who was stirring, beginning to groan.

As the girls, ignoring the dust and filth of the alley, went down on their knees beside him, he raised himself on his good elbow.

'That'd be Crane who hit me,' he said. He chuckled weakly. 'I should've known he wouldn't be far away.'

'They've gone,' said Prunella. 'George, are you all right? Are you....'

'I'm all right. Don't worry. I've got a head like a rock.'

'Your arm?'

'I didn't fall on it luckily.'

He sat up, retrieved his gun. 'They got clean away I guess.'

'Yes.'

'But they didn't get our Maria, I see.'

'No. Thanks to you, Senor George.'

He rose to his feet, Prunella's anxious hand at his elbow.

He shook his head slowly from side to side. 'Sound as a bell.'

'You are in the wars lately,' said Prunella shakily.

Things had happened with such bewildering swiftness.

The man hurtling through the window: his terrible death beneath the hooves of horses. And her father appearing in the shattered window; a sight that she would never forget; terribly bloody and battered, but unbowed – like some kind of avenger....

George was at the hotel door then and, looking through it, he must have seen something, somebody....

146

She learned later that George had spotted Lafe. And then Lafe had disappeared, going in the opposite direction. And this had led George to the alley, passing Prunella on the way, telling her to wait not to worry.

But she had not waited, for her father had grinned at her from his bloodied face and she had known he was all right and she had run into the alley.

'There's only two of 'em left it seems,' said George now, half to himself. 'I wonder what happened to Gabby.'

Walking without haste, but steadily, he led the girls up the alley to where Gabe Parker waited, swaying, surrounded by admirers, but anxious for his only daughter.

'Dad,' said Prunella, and ran to him.

Watching her, George Roddick realised that back there in the alley she had run to him too, almost in the same way. Or had he only imagined that?

He hoped it hadn't been only his imagination.

The following morning Gabe Parker was late in rising. He was stiff and sore but Doc Craven, hastening down last night after hearing about the fight, had assured him there was nothing broken anywhere, no danger of any serious damage.

'You've got the body and guts of a man ten years your junior,' said Doc bluntly. 'If you hadn't, that big fellow would've broke you in pieces.'

But the big fellow, his head caved in by an iron hoof, was well and truly deceased. There was no need to worry about him any more.

However, Gabe Parker did not try to delude himself that the ape's friend, Lafe, had gone for good.

He thought he still knew how Lafe's mind worked. Lafe would be back, and not only for the stones. Lafe had pride. Too much of it maybe. Lafe's old compadre and leader hoped that Lafe's pride, helped along by the aforesaid compadre, Gabe himself, would bring about Lafe's irrevocable fall.

Gabe dressed himself rather more slowly than usual, wincing from time to time.

He glanced at himself in the mirror and winced even harder. Decorated by strips of sticking plaster in frivolous patterns, his face was really something to make little children run and hide. He didn't know whether all that flim-flam had been necessary or whether it was just that Doc Craven's sardonic sense of humour had got the better of him.

He had a nasty blue bruise under one eye and there was something about his teeth that didn't look right – or feel right. He wondered how many of them he had lost.

He inspected his hands. The right one – the one that packed his Sunday punch – was split across the knuckles. Doc had taped it tightly. Gabe flexed his fingers, those precious fingers.

He went over to the old oak wardrobe in the corner, opened the door, delved in the back, through the hanging coats.

His old sweat-stained gunbelt hung there. He brought it out, held it in his hand, dangling from his fingers like some brown tired serpent. His mind fled back unbidden through the years and a strange exultation grew in him. But a bittersweet sadness too.

There had been the good years and the bad ones. He had met Kate and there had been less bad years. Life had been hard sometimes in their early days of marriage, and not only because money was short. For the call was still within him, the pull of the trail, the excitement, the violent nights. But that had passed and there had been peace and contentment, broken only now and then when memory was stirred by certain things: a snatch of an old border song, perhaps, mention of a certain town or place, the scent of sagebrush on the wind, a whiff of gunsmoke, the tang of cordite, the look of the sky at night when there was no moon and the stars were high and the shadows were a deep cloaking purple.

But he was older now, much older, he thought, and he could stand back from himself, as it were, and be rational about those old things. And he could admit that among the good things there had been countless bad ones. There had been hunger and cold and dirt and hate; and a running man, though he tried to tell himself different, was never really free.

So he knew now that he would do what he had to do and hope it came out all right because of his family, and for himself too, of course. But whatever he did, and however it came out – well, that was it, that was all....

He strapped on the gunbelt, flexing his fingers all the time. He found the old gun, wrapped in its oilskin in the bottom of the drawer.

He ran his hand over its black oil sheen, the cold, smooth steel; over the scarred walnut butt, almost black also with constant use.

The gun had a longer barrel than a normal Colt. It was, in fact, his old Army gun, the one he had brought away with him, together with a tattered uniform, a rifle and a horse. The gunbelt he had had made later – at a saddler's shop, he remembered: where was it? El Paso? Yes, he was sure it was El Paso....

He wondered if the little shop was still there. 'Twas said that El Paso was no longer just a dust-hole, but was growing; growing fast....

The holster? It had been with the gunbelt, of course. Specially made too, longer than usual, to take the barrel of the gun, the old Peacemaker.

It had seen some times, the old Peacemaker!

Gabe slid it into its holster. He stood in front of the long mirror in the wardrobe and made a few practise draws. His split knuckles were painful but they did not seem to impair his grip.

He was pretty fast. He wondered if he was as fast as he used to be.

But he couldn't stop to worry about that now.

He got a box of shells from the same drawer as the gun and he pressed them smoothly into the chambers.

He slid the gun back into its holster. Then he took the whole harness off again and hung it carefully over the bed rail.

He could hear Kate and Prunella moving about downstairs. He went down.

Lafe rose from before the cold ashes of the fire. Crane stretched out his legs and looked up at him.

They were both hungry and dirty.

Their talk since waking had been peevish, desultory. But Lafe had made it pretty plain what he intended to do. And now he said:

'Are you with me then?'

As was his way, Crane held off for a fragment of time before answering.

It could mean the riches they desired. Or it could mean death.

He began to get up. 'What have I got to lose?' he said.

What indeed? Nothing but his life. And that hadn't been precious to him for a long time. Not since the war. Not since his home and the plantation had been burned, his father shot, his mother driven to dementia and death. It had been a long time since he had thought of those days.

He shut them resolutely from his mind.

'Let's ride,' he said.

It seemed to him now that Lafe was a little loco, that he wanted vengeance almost more than he wanted riches. But, as always, fatalistically, Crane found himself going along with him.

TWENTY-ONE

THE LAST WALK

'You should've stayed in bed longer,' said Kate. 'I would've brought your breakfast up to you.'

'I'm later than usual anyway,' said Gabe 'I'm all right, don't you worry. I'll go get a wash and shave. I don't want any breakfast yet, just coffee. I've got some calls to make first.'

He was already on his way to the kitchen. He thought he heard Prunella say something about 'havin' a visitor for breakfast'.

When he got back, shining and fresher from his ablutions, he asked the girl about this.

'George Roddick's coming,' she said. 'I told you.'

'Did you? Well, never mind, young George won't be bothered if I'm not here to receive him. He ain't coming here to see me.'

Gabe grinned, wincing at the same time as his bruised and battered face muscles rebelled at the sudden excitement.

Prunella had nothing to say to this sally. She merely flushed and busied herself slicing bread. More bread, Gabe thought, than they'd need for the whole day, let alone break-

152

fast, visitor or no visitor.

Women were funny critturs!

'You really ought to have some breakfast, Gabe,' said Kate.

'Save it,' he said, and though he was still smiling, Kate realised he was adamant and she did not press him any further.

He did not go out right way, however, but back upstairs.

He could hear the girl, Maria, and the Gravez kids moving around. Maria had been up late last night and had been told to stay in bed longer and rest. The kids always stayed in there till the grown-ups had eaten and then everything was prepared for them and they could invade the well-loaded kitchen table. Probably they had never eaten so well before in their young lives.

Gabe went once more into his and Kate's room. He opened the wardrobe and got down on one knee. With his small clasp knife, he prised up a loose board in the base of the wardrobe and brought forth a grimy cardboard box that had once contained rifle shells.

He opened this and looked down at the uncut diamonds held in a nest of crumpled brown paper. They didn't look much. He brought the box out on to the bed and from a drawer he found more brown paper, and some string. He packed the box tighter so that the stones would not rattle about. He found notepaper and pen and ink and wrote a short note. Then he wrapped the whole thing up and tied it with string.

Old Ike down at the mail office would lend him some sealing wax, he thought, as he wrote an address on the parcel.

A little cheap-looking uninteresting parcel, which he put into the pocket of his black coat. Then, under the coat, he strapped on the gunbelt and tied the holster down with the greasy whang-string. He took more shells from the drawer and filled the tiny pouches in the belt. Then, as an after-thought, he put the rest of the shells in his pocket.

He went downstairs again.

'I won't be long,' he said.

Kate and Prunella saw the gunbelt. Neither of them made any comment, but he could feel their anxious eyes on his back as he passed through the curtain into the shop and out of their sight.

This will be the last time one way or another, he told them in his mind. I swear this.

Maybe this thing I am planning now is something I should have done years ago.

He went into the pale morning sunshine, the dusty street.

His first visit was soon concluded. Ike, the mailman, took charge of the little parcel, promised to plentifully embellish it with sealing wax and put it on the next stage, which was calling today.

Gabe knew that it would be delivered ere long to an old and trusted friend of his at the Wells Fargo office in Yellowstone.

He received old Ike's good wishes and his congratulations on the victorious battle of yesterday. Then he said So-long and went back along the street, past his own gunsmith's shop and on into the marshal's office.

Widow Webber fussed around but, sensing that Gabe wanted to talk confidentially to her patient, finally left the two men alone.

'That woman!' growled Peter Bickerston, viciously; but he couldn't help smiling as he spoke.

'She'll rope an' hogtie you yet,' said his friend.

'Don't say that, Gabe,' implored Pete. 'Don't shame the devil. I keep asking her for whiskey an' she keeps saying No. I swear she's only waitin' till I'm too thirsty and weak to resist and then she's gonna pounce on me or something.'

'Hell, you're strong enough to fight back now, aren't you?'

Pete grinned. 'I'm all right. How about you? You look like you're the one who's been kicked 'stead o' the other feller.'

'With the other feller it was fatal.'

'So I heard. Hell, I wisht I'd been there to see it. How about that feller's friends though?'

'It's them I wanted to talk to you about.'

'I figured something like that – when I saw the gun an' belt.'

'I want you to swear me in an' give me a badge, Pete.'

The marshal pointed. 'My waistcoat's hanging on the back o' the door, Gabe. There's a badge in the left-hand pocket.'

When Gabe got back to the shop George Roddick had arrived and was ploughing his way through a plate of ham and eggs with toasted rye bread on the side.

'Morning, Mr Parker,' he said, his mouth full.

'Morning, George.'

George's gaze rested momentarily on the older man's belt and gun, the silver star on his breast. But he made no comment, shovelled another large portion of food into his open mouth. Even with one hand the lean, pale kid was a formidable trencherman. His wounded arm, still in its sling, didn't seem to be bothering him none.

Gabe noted that a gunbelt was hung over the back of the young man's chair. George intercepted the older man's glance and said:

'The gun belongs to the doc. It's the one he lent me yesterday. I borrowed the gunbelt from Barnaby Jimson at the stables. He tells me he's got two of 'em.'

'Barnaby's got two of everything,' said Gabe.

It was a feeble joke and nobody laughed. Kate made a sign

to Prunella and they went into the kitchen, closing the communicating door behind them, leaving the two men alone.

Gabe said: 'I'm going after Lafe and Crane.'

George emptied his mouth, swallowing quietly. 'You don't have to,' he said. 'Fellow came in the surgery this morning from out of some ranch. Got a poisoned thumb he wanted lancing. Said he passed two fellows on the trail. Said they were a dirty, mean-looking pair. Described 'em well. It's no doubt they were Lafe and Crane. Fellow said they weren't pushing too hard, but they were coming back this way.'

George took a swig of coffee.

'They should be here any time now.' He rose and began to strap on his gunbelt.

'I had hoped it wouldn't happen in town,' said Gabe. 'But I might've figured Lafe's so eaten up with hate that he'd want a grandstand play. He's mine, George.'

'Sure.' The young man was inspecting his gun, methodically. 'I was hoping Crane wouldn't show. Crane was the only one o' the gang I could really like. Still, he knows what he wants, I guess.'

'Think you can faze him?'

'I can try.'

They were in the shop when Barnaby Jimson limped in.

'They're here,' he said. 'Just two of 'em. Need any help?'

'No. Thanks all the same, Barnaby.'

Barnaby sighed. 'I guessed you wouldn't.'

'Try and warn folks off the street, huh?'

'Will do.'

The little hostler limped and scuttled away.

'I like this town,' said George, apropos of nothing.

The two men moved out on to the boardwalk.

They saw Lafe and Crane right away. Goaded by hate, and greed too, Lafe wasn't wasting any time, Gabe thought.

What did those two intend to do with the diamonds, even if they got them, he wondered; where would they find a buyer? It seemed to him that the stones were just a sort of symbol now, that, diamonds or no diamonds, Lafe and he had been, over the years, walking inevitably towards this time, towards this meeting on a dusty street in the pale morning sunshine.

It was a great pity that they should have had to bring others with them – to bring young George at least. The others, Crane, would have finished this way somewhere, on some other street, sometime anyway.

He was a killer, a professional. But young George wasn't; not really. Even if he was as fast as he thought, was that fast enough to beat an old timer like Crane?

He was brave, laconic.

Gabe feared for him.

He wondered whether George, despite his steady demeanour, was a mite nervous. Nervousness could make a man over-hasty, spoil his aim. Gabe said softly with a smile:

'You rate a star, boy.'

'Forget it.'

'Consider yourself well an' truly sworn in.'

'Sure. Me – a lawman!'

'Me too!'

'Yeh. Me still a thief though. What about the stones?'

'They're already on their way back to Wells Fargo. To one of their agents in Yellowstone, an old friend who I'd trust with my life. He'll see they reach the appropriate quarter, an' no questions asked.'

'You think of everything, don't you?' said George. But there was a chuckle in his voice.

There was a rapport between these two men, the young and the middle-aged.

They both hoped it would not be broken.

'Let's go,' said George.

They stepped off the boardwalk into the dusty street.

Lafe and Crane were already on the street, moving forward, walking slowly. They were beginning to part a bit, to fan out. Now Gabe and George, by tacit agreement, a nod, a glance, began to do the same.

'*Vaya Con Dios*,' said Gabe softly. The old border goodbye that was not a goodbye. Nobody heard him but himself.

The gap narrowed. There was nobody on the street except the four men. Indistinct faces appeared at windows. Gabe Parker noted that the two other men, old hands, had arranged things so that the sun was at their backs. Luckily, it was not yet a brilliant sun.

Lafe must be very eager, Gabe reflected. It would have been more like him to stage the fight in the brilliant heat of midday when the sun was glaring. Or at night, his natural element, when the shadows were deep.

But the gap was still narrowing and now Gabe concentrated wholly on Lafe the person, here and now, knowing that George was keeping level, step by step with him, walking to his own deadly rendezvous with his old friend, Crane.

It was a pity, a mockery, that old friends (and hadn't Lafe been his, Gabe's, friend once too?) should have to meet ultimately this way.

But it was too late to turn back now. There was never any turning back.

Keep your mind on your business, Gabe, he told himself: you may have to take Crane too.

He pushed the thought from his mind. Time enough....

Time was running out. The gap was narrower still. Gabe

noted that the false front of the Seven Spot Saloon cast a long shadow. That shadow was in just the right position, it would take the sunlight out of his and George's eyes.

You're slipping, Lafe boy, he thought. But you're fast and expert and I'm older and somewhat out of practice. For the first time he looked directly at Lafe's face over the narrow gap.

The lean, pale face black with a few days' growth of beard, the eyes staring a little, savage as a loco wolf's. The fancy clothes now travel-stained, the Stetson battered, hiding the silver slash in the black hair.

There was nothing in this animal, this killer that reminded him of the young Lafe he had known so many years ago.

Gabe was bareheaded, as George was bareheaded. Gabe felt the cool morning breeze on his face coming in off the plains.

The shadows bathed his face now and he watched Lafe's eyes, saw the tell-tale flicker even in their pale deadness. Lafe moved.

God, he *was* fast.

But Gabe felt his body going through the age-old motions, cleanly, smoothly.

He thumbed the hammer and the gun bucked satisfyingly in his hand, tingling his palm, roaring.

The street was suddenly full of gunfire.

Lafe was still upright, but Gabe knew he did not have to fire again. Lafe could not raise his unfired gun any higher. He seemed to be trying to say something to Gabe. But no sound came. His eyes became blank, black. With a convulsive jerk, he pitched forward on his face in the dust.

Gabe pivoted, his gun covering Crane, who reclined, resting on one elbow on the ground.

'Don't shoot,' said George Roddick, hoarsely.

Crane's gun was still in his hand, but it lowered gently to the dust.

George said: 'He could've killed me. He's faster … faster. He hesitated at the last moment.'

They went over to the man.

Crane looked up at George. 'Goddamn you, you crazy young fool,' he growled.

His shoulder was shattered, blood sopping his shirt. He smiled crookedly and then rolled over on to his back and lapsed into unconsciousness.

People moved into the street.

Barnaby Jimson reached the two men first. The small, crippled hostler moved with incredible swiftness.

He looked down at Crane and shook his head slowly from side to side. 'A strange man,' he said.

'See that he's taken care of,' said Gabe. 'That his wound's looked after, he's fed. When he's fit give him what he needs and let him ride.'

'I'll do that, Gabe.'

Lafe lay on his face, his dead fingers clawing at the rutted dirt of the street.

The message was written there years ago, thought Gabe, written in the dust.

It was better than finishing at the end of a rope anyway.

Gabe turned away. George moved again to his side.

They walked back towards the gunsmith's shop, to the doorway where the two women stood awaiting them.

160